MURDER IS MURDER IS MURDER

SAMUEL M. STEWARD

ALYSON PUBLICATIONS

This is a paperback original from Alyson Publications, Inc., PO Box 2783, Boston, MA 02208. Distributed in England by Gay Men's Press, PO Box 247, London, N15 6RW.

First edition, May 1985   5 4 3 2 1

ISBN 0 932870 68 6

FOR MARTIN
whose natal day,
though not the same year,
follows Gertrude's by one

Contents

❧ I ❧

A Faun in the Garden

"ROSEMARY, PUSSY," GERTRUDE YELLED as she hove into Alice's sacred sanctuary of the kitchen, brandishing a fistful of greenery above her head. She shook it enthusiastically. "Guess where I found it, down by the river in the loam, growing wild and I got my shoes muddy."

Alice finished polishing the bottom of a large copper pan, and set it down on the big thick butcher-block table on which the kitchen murders took place, for it was there that she slaughtered and disemboweled the fowls and doves that made their meals.

"That's dandy, just dandy," she said, brushing her bangs down over the cyst on her forehead, whence they had been dislodged by her exuberant polishing. "But did it ever occur to you, Lovey, to look over in the corner of the garden where rosemary and thyme and tarragon are taking over the place? There's bushels."

Gertrude was crestfallen. "And I thought you'd be so pleased."

"Oh, I am dear, I am. Probably it's more flavorful, coming from the river's loam down there," she said.

"What's for dinner," Gertrude asked. She never used question marks. They were fine for brands on cattle, and commas helped you put on your overcoat — but they were all useless in speaking and writing. Her questions were inflected to fall at the end, not rise. Some listeners were confused.

"Roasted squab with wild rice, a deviled sauce of shallots in white wine, a salad with oil and tarragon vinegar and a wee bit of chopped truffle from the one that Monsieur Dardaine's pig got out for us."

"Is that all," said Gertrude.

"By no means," said Alice. "Tiny green peas with herbs, tiny new potatoes from the garden with mint and parsley, and fresh strawberries with raspberry sauce and whipped cream. And wine."

"What's the big occasion," Gertrude demanded.

Alice looked hurt. "Just to show I love you," she said.

"Me as well as good food," said Gertrude.

"That too," said Alice.

Gerturde leaned on the butcher block, supported by one hand. "Well, I'm tired that's wot I am and I'm going up to take my forty winks and Chen can call me about twenty minutes before you're ready. And I don't want any wine. It gives me the bellyache."

Alice nodded, whipping sauce in a wooden bowl.

Gertrude stomped noisily up the stone stairs to their bedroom, and lay down heavily on their marriage bed, taking off her muddy sandals before she fell on the quilted coverlet, one she had brought all the way from the States to Bilignin in southern France. Soon she snored.

A small part of the world knew Gertrude Stein as the grand-mother [she was sixty-three in that year of 1937] of avant-garde American literature, the influencer of the styles of Hemingway, Anderson and many others, the practitioner of arcane and hermetic [and some said automatic] writing, and the light of the world to her lover-companion Alice B. Toklas. A few of the world knew she adored reading murder mysteries, but not many knew that she and Alice had solved several murders themselves: the forgery and murder at the Louvre, the mystery of the verger who died defending the weeping Madonna, the weeping willow crime, and the disastrous Hollywood scandal of the starlet's death.

Currently she was *en bloc*, as the French say — a writer's block had descended on her, and nothing seemed able to remove it. She would sit with her pen in hand, the French schoolboy's notebook with its blank ruled pages in front of her, and think and think and think until her forehead began to sweat small drops of blood, almost, although she knew that it was really only perspiration. Even the mysterious death of Madame Pernollet, the hotel-keeper's wife over in Belley, had not been able to get her started on a murder mystery which she dearly wanted to write, especially since she thought she had a wonderful title for it, *Blood on the Dining Room Floor.*

Every time Gertrude developed a block — which luckily was not often — she had feelings akin, she believed, to those of a person who had just opened his veins by slicing his wrists. She wanted *la gloire*, lots of it, and she had written for thirty years before she had a taste of it. Then by pretending that a book she wrote had been the autobiography of Alice, she made her mark. She was lioness-ized on her trip to America in 1934, and they both loved every minute and second of it — the bright handsome students, the old girl friends, the professors, the police, the airplanes — from which looking down she was reminded of cubism and French art. They loved the crowds in Hollywood, that murder that she and Alice solved — oh, millions and millions of things, all stored in the back of Gertrude's brain, to be called upon when next she wrote . . . what a wonderful experience! Except that now, alas, it had all dried up. Withered, by God. Dammed. Stopped. Ceased. Terminé.

Half-dozing after a few minutes of deep sleep, she came awake, her big heavy frame indenting the bed. Downstairs she heard Alice still beating something in a bowl. A far-off cowbell tinkled. Locusts sang their monotone somewhere outside. A cart rumbled over cobblestones.

She stretched her arms upward, almost as if she were imploring the deity, and let them fall.

"Ah, la gloire!" she murmured, turned over on her side, and began to snore again. Her last conscious thought: "Damn that Hemingway."

From the kitchen window Alice peered into the garden, looking with approval at the freshly trimmed box hedges with their lustrous leaves, and at the pile of weeds which young Pierre Desjardins had gathered together. What a handsome young man! A yellow-haired stalwart, bare to the waist. His skin glistened with sweat, the muscles arranged in a landscape of perfection — all hillocks and valleys, brown and beautiful, each moving, rising and falling, as he worked the hoe — and then, stooping for a few last weeds, his magnificent thighs revealed under the pale blue thin fabric of his work pants, his biceps swelling, the muscles in his forearms answering the movement of his hands.

"Even though I am in love with Lovey," she murmured, "I can still adore beauty, no matter what or where."

It was such a pity that such a beautiful young animal had been damaged from birth. He was a deaf-mute, *un sourd-muet*. She talked with him only in sign language — no lip-reading — and she was the only one in Bilignin who had mastered it besides his father. Her thin hands when she signed metamorphosed into butterflies, into quick darting hummingbirds, flicking and fluttering, pausing and pointing. It was easy, for Alice in her youth had been an accomplished pianist.

Alice remembered that before they had hired the young man to come to work for them once a week, Gertrude and she had had a long discussion about him. Alice, who rarely forgot anything, remembered it word for word . . .

"I don't like it, I don't like it at all," Gertrude had said.

"What now, Lovey?" asked Alice.

"That you should be the only one able to talk to him. You know how I like to talk, to neighbors and everybody else. It's one of the ways I get the ideas for my writing, and I'm mad because I can't talk to him."

"Just tell me what you want and I'll ask him all the questions," Alice said.

"Well then. Ask him about his father Grand Pierre, and is the old man going to be married again ever, and what does he think of school and what's he going to do later for a living and things like that."

Alice sighed. "He's such a beautiful young man. That face and body. So pure. Better than the David. Or Antinoüs. I think I could almost love him."

"So could I," said Gertrude. "We must be turning queer."

"Oh say not so," Alice giggled. "Perish forbid."

"And that body, good grief, he must be two meters tall."

"One eighty-three," said Alice. "I asked him."

"But it's still something I don't like," said Gertrude petulantly. "You being the only one able to talk to him."

"You could learn, Lovey."

Gertrude looked at her thick-fingered hands. "I'm too clumsy," she said. "And lazy. I might as well admit it." Then she looked thoughtful. "I wonder what his voice is, I wonder."

"He has no voice," said Alice. "I've never heard it. It must be a screech."

"Do you think he's . . . *of it.*"

"Nothing matters," Alice said smiling. "The damaged vessels make up for it in other ways. He could be a man or woman."

"Just look at him," said Gertrude. "He's a man."

"I have been looking," said Alice.

"His father is over-protective. A tyrant."

"But that one's not so bad-looking himself," said Alice. "With that farmer's body, his big hands, his small . . . er . . . derrière."

"Hey, none of that," said Gertrude scowling.

"You've had *your* fling," said Alice, somewhat bitterly. "Why not I? You've looked at Madeleine Rops. And Suzanne. Why shouldn't I have a little lust of the eye?"

"Because you're mine and and I'm yours and that's all there is to it and has been for thirty years and will be longer I hope and you do too."

Alice said, "You're sweet."

"I will have to admit," said Gertrude, "that of all the people in Bilignin the boy's the best looking and everything else. I wonder what country wench will get him, I wonder, probably some buck-toothed slut from over the hill or some spindly boy, I suppose he's already been initiated, with those looks he can't help but be."

"Yes," said Alice, "but there are fewer than twenty people in Bilgnin so he doesn't have many rivals to go up against."

"Nevertheless," said Gertrude.

Alice went on. "That father of his is very jealous of him in a funny kind of way, I mean about letting him out. And with the mother dead . . ."

"What'd she die of," Gertrude asked.

"Some mysterious disease. She glowed in the dark for several days after."

"Good grief," said Gertrude. "What in the world of."

Alice shrugged. "Some medicine she was taking. Poison. Maybe phosphorus. For bone marrow."

"The father *is* nice," said Gertrude.

"Terribly hot-tempered," said Alice. "Once when he stepped on a rake and it banged him on the head he got so mad he broke it all to smithereens, handle and all."

"Tsk," said Gertrude.

"Raised with a father like that," Alice said, "who won't let him go out ever, except on Saturday evenings when he plays *boules* in the village, and then papa goes along to see he doesn't get into trouble or speak to any of the girls."

"He's certainly going to be one of us, looks like," said Gertrude.

"Maybe," said Alice. "But he's managed to get Pauline of Belley all wound up."

Gertrude harrumphed. "She's a tart. She'd get wound up over anything with a dangler."

"Don't be vulgar, dearie," said Alice.

"Will if I want to," said Gertrude, and stomped out of the kitchen.

Alice sighed, thinking how Gertrude always managed to get the last word, and went on with her beating.

❧ II ❧

Small Troubles Here and There

THERE APPEARED IN THE KITCHEN DOORWAY a faun in pale trousers, bare to the waist and smiling.

Alice put down her bowl. "So soon?" she signed at him.

"Yes," he signed. His strong brown fingers began to flash. "The box hedge is all trimmed and everything is finished. I can't do much with the roses yet," he said. "The bushes should not be trimmed until the first of the year. But I will come then and do it, while you are in Paris."

Alice's fingers flickered. "You're a dear boy," she signed, and then: "How are you getting on? Will you be going back to your special school this fall?"

"If I can persuade my father," he signed. "He wants me to stay to help with the chores around the house. Things like milking the cows and feeding them, and tending the vines. You know — what's necessary in the vineyard."

The sign for "milking" disturbed Alice a little. It reminded her of other things.

"Of course," she signed. "And are you happy now?"

A frown drifted across his clear forehead, and was gone

like a summer cloud. "Oh yes," he said, but his fingers moved slowly.

"Is something wrong?"

He shook his head, but looked down and turned his right toe into the dirt. "My father," he said — and his signing was slow. "He is having a quarrel with Monsieur Debat."

Alice made a sign of impatience, and then agreement. "Never mind," she signed. "Everyone quarrels with Debat. What is it about?"

Again the young man looked down. "I do not exactly know. It has to do with something that belongs to father."

Alice approached him and patted his shoulder. His skin was warm, and moist. "Never mind," she said again. "It will pass. I do wish that Debat would move somewhere else to live. No one likes him."

The young man sighed, while his fingers made an intricate pattern.

"Alas, he cannot do that. His wife is dead and he will stay in Bilignin. Like my father, with mother dead too. Without a wife he also does not want to move. We must live on the land, like Debat."

"Ah yes," Alice signed. "You with your vineyards and he with his crops. It is too bad."

"We cannot give them up," the young man said. "No more than he. All Frenchmen love the land."

"You will learn to live in peace and be happy," said Alice.

The boy looked down again, while his fingers, near his crotch, said, "It is my hope."

"Go then," Alice signed, "and have contentment. Will you be here next week as usual?"

"Of course," the young man said.

"Then I would like you to weed the front of the château, and paint the iron gate."

"Understood," the young man said, his face breaking into a smile.

Alice patted his shoulder again. "And not to worry," she signed. "Everything will be all right."

"Perhaps," the boy said. He picked up his implements and turned to go, smiling at Alice and flicking a goodbye at his forehead.

She watched him down the path — his lithe body gracefully moving, the hoe over his naked shoulder, the small trim derrière, the lean strong thighs tightly enclosed in the blue trousers. His back muscles did a slow and gentle trepak as he moved. Halfway down the path he put down his bucket and shifted the hoe to the other shoulder, then picked up the bucket in his other hand. His back was burned to a dark sienna, and there was a light patch of hair disappearing down beneath his waistline. All in all, it was a most beautifully muscled body, and Alice sighed.

"My God," she said. "It's pure beauty, that one. If I weren't the way I was, or if I were a fairy, I'd get him before sundown, come hell or high water." She sighed, and went back into the chatêu.

A little later Gertrude came downstairs and into the kitchen. She yawned mightily. She had put on a burlap skirt, and wore a pink chiffon blouse with belled sleeves over which was a quilted yellow sleeveless vest. Her light woolen stockings went well with brown sandals. Her short Roman haircut had one cowlick sticking up behind. She rarely used a comb on her hair, simply using her hand to smooth it forward, so that the Roman senator look took less than any trouble at all.

"Couldn't really sleep," she announced.

"Pity," said Alice.

"Has P'tit Pierre gone yet," she asked.

"He left about a half hour ago."

"Damnit, I wish I could talk to him the way you do."

"So you've said several times," said Alice. "But why? He doesn't have much to say, and I can tell him everything about the garden. And you could learn the sign language if you wanted to."

"I'm too fumble-fingered," Gertrude said. "And anyway you know how I like to talk to people and have people talk to me. I want to know everything about everyone and to hear them out loud. I want to know about him and his father, do you suppose they have anything to do with each other, how do they get along with the mother dead, who does the sewing and cooking, certainly I would like to know that, and when I don't know it is a bother."

Alice sighed. "You've told me all this before," she said.

"I know," said Gertrude. "That's the way my brain works."

"It is a sign of senility," said Alice.

"It is not," said Gertrude firmly. "Don't you remember the *Hunting of the Snark*, he said if I tell you a thing three times you'll know it is true."

"All right," Alice said. "The next time I'll ask him all those things."

"It ain't like talking direct," Gertrude muttered.

"Come to think of it, there *is* something about P'tit Pierre," Alice said, resting both hands on the stove which was cold at the moment.

Gertrude was excited. "What is it, tell me at once, now what was it. There's not much to talk about around here until the guests come and you know how I like gossip, and you and me, we have about worn ourselves out with talk, and when do the next come anyway."

"Johnny McAndrews is due in two weeks. And Cecil Beaton and Francis Rose some time after."

"Those two fairies," said Gertrude with mild disdain.

"Now, now, Lovey," Alice said. "Don't speak ill of your pilgrims and disciples. Or of yourself for that matter."

"Humph," Gertrude said. "Females ain't fairies, all fairies are males."

"Even Titania?" Alice asked.

Gertrude chose to ignore that. "Tell me what's the matter with Petit Pierre, go ahead and tell."

"Well, something's bothering him," Alice said. "He had a kind of hangdog look, as if something had gone wrong or he had been hurt in some way."

"How could you tell all that from his fingers."

"Hell," said Alice. "With a deaf-mute you just don't depend on fingers. With even anybody you look at everything. There's body language added. I got it from that. From his gestures. He dug his toe in the dirt, for one thing. He looked down, for another. You read all those things together. Something's happened to him that he didn't want to tell. Or at any rate, something he didn't tell."

"We'll have to find out," said Gertrude. "Somehow."

Alice nodded wisely. "We will, Lovey. We will."

❧ III ❧

A Chance They Missed

GERTRUDE AND ALICE LOVED the corner of France where they spent their summers and autumns. There seemed to be more sky in the province of Ain than anywhere else in France, and the air was cooler and cleaner. One day ten years before, they had been touring the area, and had looked across a broad and fertile valley to see an old château with a low retaining wall.

"I must live there," said Gertrude.

"There may be a problem," said Alice. "I see curtains blowing in the breeze. It is evidently inhabited."

"Nevertheless," said Gertrude.

It was indeed inhabited, by an army officer who had no intention of moving. But when Gertrude and Alice went back to Paris, they spoke a word here and there to various friends, with the result that the astonished army officer found himself suddenly promoted and stationed at a faraway post. And Gertrude and Alice shortly thereafter moved into the old château at Bilignin.

It was an ideal spot for them. There was a small formal garden with boxwood hedges surrounding a few flower plots, and from the garden and the windows they could see over the low wall across a dim and misty wooded valley to a circle of blue hills, with Mont Blanc in the distance. The house itself on the other side was guarded by a high wall with an iron gate. When they moved in they modernized the old château somewhat, with a new hot water system and a new stove in the kitchen. The rest of the house stayed pretty much as it was, and once Johnny McAndrews — with a dampened cloth and some careful pulling — discovered that the wallpaper went back, layer by layer, through the Revolution and the Empire to the time of Louis XVI. The high ceilinged downstairs salon had trompe l'oeil decorations of hunting-horns and corbeilles of fruits, and there Gertrude had her favorite ancient rocking-chair to sit in, a kind of throne that was for her use alone.

To the old château, then, came an endless stream of visitors and pilgrims, some to pay homage to Gertrude, and others who were old friends. And there the two of them stayed with their two dogs, Basket and Pepe, from April through October, entertaining the guests who made the trip from Paris to see them.

Gertrude and Alice were well-enough liked by the five families in the hamlet of Bilignin, and by many of the persons in nearby Belley. But there were two, a man and a woman, whom neither Gertrude nor Alice could abide.

One was Mademoiselle Guerre, an ancient turkey-buzzard of a woman who in medieval times would have been branded a witch. She lived in Belley, and so was removed from the path of Gertrude and Alice by three kilometers.

The other was Monsieur Debat, and with him they

were not so lucky. He was a husky evil-tempered good-looking man in his forties, but everyone referred to him as Old Debat. He had some acreage down in the valley below their château, and to get to it he had to pass along a path that took him into their view each morning. At first both Gertrude and Alice had tried to speak to him, with a pleasant "Bonjour." But receiving nothing from him save a grunt or a stare, they soon abandoned all pretense to friendliness. And they also discovered that everyone in Bilignin hated Old Debat, and that he was especially loathed by the father of young Pierre Desjardins — Grand Pierre to the villagers, whereas the handsome son was called Petit Pierre, although he was a few centimeters taller than his father.

It was a clear crisp Monday morning, and the dew still lay heavy on the hedges and the rose bushes in the garden. Alice, with a pair of shears, was trimming some plants that she had forbidden P'tit Pierre to touch. With her small bent figure (she was sixty that year), her bangs and faint mustache, she looked as if she belonged in such a garden forever.

She peered over the low retaining wall, far down into the flat lowland of the valley. Old Debat had already started his ploughing, and followed behind the horse that dragged the blade. He was so far away, near the edge of his field where it ended in trees and an undergrowth, that Alice could barely make him out.

"Basta!" she said with a Jamesian fervor, and was about to get on with her pruning, when she saw another figure at the far end of the field, a man, walking rapidly toward Old Debat.

"I wonder who . . ." Alice said, and then sprinted quickly across the garden to the salon. She went inside the tall door and picked up the spyglass from the clavichord.

Then she went speedily back across the garden, pulling the telescope to its proper length, all leather and brass joinings, and uncovered the eyepiece. It was a favorite of hers, and she much preferred it to Gertrude's excellent binoculars.

But it was hard to handle — about a meter long, and it jiggled in her grasp. She knelt by the retaining wall and balanced the spyglass on the rough stone. The figure of the horse and Monsieur Debat jumped into brilliant clarity. Moving the telescope a bit to the right, she saw the other figure hurrying down the length of the field. One arm was raised — who was it? She blinked, and finally identified him. It was Grand Pierre.

He was now half-running toward Debat, who had stopped the horse and was looking behind.

"Good fathers!" Alice said out loud. She was about to witness a confrontation. Her excitement made the spyglass jiggle more nervously than ever. Lovey would never forgive her for not calling her to watch.

Alice hurried back into the house and shouted up the stairs.

"Come Lovey, quick!" she yelled. "Bring the binoculars. Hurry!"

"What," yelled Gertrude.

"Hurry!" Alice called. "We may witness a confrontation."

"What," yelled Gertrude again.

"Damn that deafness," Alice muttered, and tried once more. But she had to repeat it again after that. Then without waiting longer she dashed into the garden again, knelt by the wall, and brought the spyglass into play once more. There was no one there except Debat. The horse had turned at the forested end of the field and was started on a new furrow back in the direction toward Alice and the château. She looked at Debat's face — a hard and cruel face. He seemed to be red and sweating — but then again, why not? The sun was out in full hot ball, and ploughing was strenuous work.

But where was Grand Pierre?

Gertrude came hastily out of the house, carrying the binoculars. "What is it, Pussy, what in the world is it."

Alice turned and shrugged. "Nothing now, I guess," she said. "I just saw Monsieur Desjardins, Grand Pierre, hurrying toward Old Debat, looking as if he were itching for a fight. But by the time I got back after calling you, Debat was all alone and ploughing as if nothing had happened."

"Where did Grand Pierre go," Gertrude asked.

"A mystery," said Alice. "Maybe into the woods. The path through them leads to Belley, after all, though it's roundabout."

"I wonder why Grand Pierre seemed to be so mad at Debat," Gertrude said.

"Another mystery," said Alice. "Perhaps some time I can find out from P'tit Pierre."

"When will the young man come to work again," Gertrude asked.

"Day after tomorrow," Alice said.

"I'll eavesdrop while you ask him. Or should I say eaveslook. Where did that damn word come from anyway."

"From standing under the eaves to listen at an open window," said Alice. "Perhaps."

"Pitter patter," Gertrude said.

"Petit Pierre," said Alice.

"Stop it," Gertrude said, "or you'll start me up again. This time with a P."

❀ IV ❀

Where, Oh Where?

BUT IT WAS SOONER THAN the "day after tomorrow" that they were to see Petit Pierre.

Alice was at the garden wall the next afternoon, using a twig to prod the snails that moved their small houses slowly along. With a practiced flick of her wrist she upended them and watched them sail through the air, to land on the hillside some ten feet below. The grey stone of the wall was covered with their pearly glistening tracks, crystalline in the sunlight. On her head she wore one of Gertrude's high-crowned straw hats.

I am essentially not a cruel person, she thought — but these damned beasts have got to go.

Suddenly there was a fearful clamor from the front of the house. She recognized it for what it was. There was no doorbell at the great iron gate that led into the small yard in front of the château, but she had thoughtfully suspended a small iron bar on a rope nearby. An arriving visitor — if he had enough sense to figure out what to do ["and if he hasn't," said Alice to Gertrude, "then I think we would not be interested in speaking to him in the first place"] — could simply take up the bar and rattle it against the bars of the gate. The resulting racket was loud enough to startle all the people who lived in the hamlet.

Alice recognized the identity of the racketeer before she could hasten to her. Three short and a long. "It's Mademoiselle Delarue," she said to herself.

And so it was — but beside her was Petit Pierre, clad in his same tight blue pants and wearing a shirt, the sleeves of which were rolled high on his upper arms. Mademoiselle Delarue was a flaming-cheeked bosomy woman, with breasts that had sagged a good deal. Her hair was twisted into a tight bun on top of her head, and she wore an apron over her dun-colored skirt.

"Bonjour, Mademoiselle," said the stout woman.

"Bonjour, Mademoiselle Delarue," said Alice, drawing back the tricky bolt which fastened the iron gate — two inches to the right, down a notch, then an inch to the left. A stranger could scarcely have mastered the device in a half hour. "What brings you here this morning?"

Mademoiselle Delarue spoke rapidly and volubly in the peasant French of the region of Ain. "We seem to be having some trouble," she declared. "Petit Pierre came this morning and wrote me a note, since there is no one in the village who can finger-speak to him except you and his father. And—" she waved a piece of paper in the air — "Pierre says that his father has disappeared, that he did not come home at all last night."

Alice was startled. Grand Pierre was a sober man, scarcely one to run around chasing women, and certainly not given to alcohol in vast amounts.

She looked at Petit Pierre and her fingers flashed into immediate action, translating aloud for Mademoiselle's benefit as she signed to the young man.

"Oh Pierre," she said. "I am sorry to hear this. Has your father ever done this before?"

Pierre's fingers were unsteady as he replied, "Never before without telling me."

"When did you see him last?"

"Yesterday morning," the youth signed. "He was going to walk into Belley to buy some things."

"To walk?" Alice asked. "Why did he not take the bicyclette?"

"It has a bad wheel," said Pierre. "That was one of the reasons he was going to Belley, to get the parts that were broken. And to buy some nails and bread and supplies at the store."

"What time was this?"

"He left very early — about eight o'clock."

"That's very odd — strange," Alice signed, speaking her words at the same time for Mademoiselle Delarue's benefit, "For I saw him down in the valley, in old Debat's field, about ten-thirty yesterday morning. I thought he was going to Belley then. He seemed to be headed in that direction."

"Perhaps he has a lady-friend in Belley," Mademoiselle Delarue interposed.

Alice added the statement to her fingers.

"No," said young Pierre. "That is, I do not think that he does. I think that perhaps he would have told me if he had."

"Fathers often do not tell their sons such things," Alice said, smiling above her rapid fingers.

Petit Pierre smiled a little weakly in return.

At that moment Gertrude rounded the corner of the house. "What's going on," she asked. "I heard voices. Bonjour Mademoiselle, bonjour Pierre."

Alice conveyed the greeting, and Pierre signed "Bonjour."

Then Alice quickly told Gertrude about the disappearance.

"What time was it we saw him, or rather you saw him, down in the valley," Gertrude asked.

"About ten-thirty."

Gertrude jammed her hands deeply into her skirt pockets, her feet apart, stretching her homespun skirt tightly.

"Humm," she said. "It is a mystery." Alice's fingers flickered briefly.

Then there was silence. A cowbell tinkled up the hill. Some locusts whirred nearby.

"What shall we do?" asked Mademoiselle Delarue. "Do you think that we ought to notify the police?"

"Perhaps not right away. There may be some good reason," Gertrude said, while Alice's fingers moved almost too fast to follow. "Why don't we wait until tomorrow and if he doesn't show up, then by all means let us notify the gendarmes, they will know what to do and maybe where to look."

"But he has never done anything like this before," Pierre signed.

"Did he have any other business to attend to in Belley," Gertrude asked.

"Anything with a doctor, a lawyer perhaps?" Mademoiselle Delarue asked.

Alice was kept busy, and then added on her own: "Did he tell you what time he might be returning?"

The young man shook his head. "No doctors or lawyers. Just going to the stores. And he said he'd be back by noon."

Then both Gertrude and Mademoiselle Delarue started to talk at once — a colloquy with one holding for an immediate notification of the gendarmerie in Belley, another wanting to tell the mayor, and both of them wondering if he had been seen anywhere, on the road, near the caserne where the Sénégalese troops were stationed, in Belley or where, what stores he had gone to, what he had purchased, whether they ought to consult the psychic Madame Rosier . . .

Alice finally threw up her hands, unable to do all the translating and signing at the same time when they were talking so rapidly.

"We shall wait," she announced. And to Pierre: "Go home, dear boy, and perhaps he will show up with a reasonable explanation." To Mademoiselle Delarue she bade goodbye, and said in English to Gertrude, "Come, Lovey, let's go in."

Gertrude shook hands with the two, and shut the gate with a loud clang. Her eyes were sparkling. "It's a mystery, that's what it is, and do you think we'll solve it now do you."

"Grand Pierre will probably solve it by showing up today," said Alice shortly.

And then, as they went around the house to the garden, she said, shaking the fingers of both hands loosely from the wrist, "Good fathers, I feel like a child again."

"Why's that," asked Gertrude.

"My fingers haven't had so much exercise since I used to practice three hours on the piano. At the university. I'm worn out."

Gertrude snorted mildly. "It's good for you," she said.

Alice tossed her head. "It's as bad as typing *The Making of Americans*," she said.

"Both of them," said Gertrude, "will keep you from getting arthritis."

❧ V ❧

Confessio Victimis

THE NEXT MORNING GERTRUDE CAME downstairs much earlier than usual, and dared once more to set foot into the kitchen, paying no attention to Alice's momentary scowl at such an invasion of her queendom.

"Have you heard anything yet," she demanded.

"Not a word," said Alice, dicing a stalk of celery.

"Tell you what," said Gertrude in her heartiest manner. "Why don't you fix me up one of your nice breakfast trays on the good silver platter, the way you do for the guests, and bring it out into the garden so I can look at Mont Blanc and eat it."

"Eat Mont Blanc?" said Alice, who loved to tease her. "You must watch your weight."

"You know what I mean," Gertrude said.

"You must say what you mean," said Alice. "You are always saying one must not be haunted by the spoken word, and this morning you seem to be spooked about it."

"Nevertheless," said Gertrude. "I think it's too early to be playing word games, and anyway you ought to fix me the breakfast, you ought to be getting in practice for Johnny when he comes next week."

"I'll do it," Alice said, "but I haven't got time to polish the platter. You'll have to eat it tarnished."

"Eat what tarnished," Gertrude asked. "Now who's not saying what they mean."

Alice raised the slicing knife formidably. "Go sit in the garden," she said. "It will be ready soon."

Beaming hugely at her, Gertrude retreated to the garden and sat down rather heavily in the lounge chair. In the early mornings the château shaded the little formal box-hedged plots, and it was very comfortable. She surveyed her summer landscape — all blue and still a little misty from the night fog that rose in the valleys sometimes until it seemed the château was floating on a pale sea. Mont Blanc was visible to the northeast. It would be a fine day.

In a little while Alice came from the château, bearing the meter-long oval silver tray with the silver coffeepot on it, steaming, and a large white cup and saucer with pale blue designs alongside a gleaming white napkin and a small jug of milk. There was a pot of fresh butter, softened to the consistency that Gertrude liked, and another small pot of red currant jam. Under the silver dome of the warmer — which Gertrude at once lifted — were two golden croissants.

"Only two, why not three," Gertrude asked.

"That's all you get," said Alice. "I'm going to keep you below eighty-five kilos this summer or know the reason why."

"Bosh," said Gertrude. "Eating's one of the two pleasures left."

"And the other?"

Gertrude looked at her, twinkling. "Writing, of course."

"Humph," said Alice. "Be careful. The milk's poisoned." She retreated into the house.

Gertrude ate slowly and quietly, savoring the rich country butter as it melted on the hot croissants. Just as she finished the last of the fragrant coffee — strong enough this morning to raise the hairs on her neck — the front gate began its clattering once again.

She listened. Then yelled, "Oh Pussy, it's Petit Pierre at the gate."

"I know!" shouted Alice from the kitchen.

"Bring him into the garden," Gertrude shouted. "I want to watch him talk."

She heard the clang of the gate as Alice opened it and then bolted it again, and soon the two of them came around the corner of the château into the garden. Pierre was wearing a pearl grey shirt and his pale blue trousers. His yellow curls were tousled by the breeze, and he looked a shade lighter than he had yesterday, a kind of beige dullness beneath his tan.

"He's not come back yet," said Alice. "And Pierre asks if he ought not go to the police. I told him that we would go along right now, and drive him in the Matford into Belley. After all, we are perhaps the last ones to see his father. So far."

"You mean you were," said Gertrude. "I didn't."

"Whatever," said Alice. She signed to Pierre to sit on the low garden wall, and she sat beside him. Then she began to talk to him, her fingers flying.

"There was no word of any kind?" she asked him.

His face was troubled, and he shook his head.

"You know that we saw your father down in the valley

in Debat's field yesterday," she told him. "About ten-thirty in the morning."

"Yes," Pierre's fingers said. "But I cannot understand. He left for Belley much earlier than that."

"Perhaps he had already been to Belley and was coming back."

"Pussy," Gertrude said sharply. "Will you please translate out loud. I want to hear everything."

"Sorry, Lovey," said Alice. "I forgot —" and she repeated what she had learned from Pierre.

Gertrude entered the conversation. "What direction was he headed when he was in Debat's field," she asked, and Alice's fingers posed the question which she herself had to answer: "In the direction of Belley, toward the forest."

"That's odd," said Gertrude. "Was he carrying anything, packages or a filet with what he had bought if he had been there."

Alice closed her eyes momentarily, thinking. "Yes," she said, opening them. "He had a package under one arm — no, I think he was carrying a filet. One of those net shopping bags. With his free arm — well, he was shaking his fist at Debat."

Gertrude looked at Pierre. "Why was your father mad at old Debat," she asked, and Alice's fingers flickered.

A curious thing happened. Pierre looked away so that he could not see Alice's fingers. In effect, he had cut himself out of the conference — no longer able to see or hear or speak. After a moment he scuffed the gravel near the garden wall with one foot. Finally his fingers began to move.

Alice was silent. She watched him intently.

"What —" Gertrude began, but Alice held up a hand to silence her. "Just a moment until I get it all," she whispered.

Pierre delivered himself of quite a long narrative. His face flushed and then paled. He looked down at the gravel again, sighed, and finally looked directly at Alice, then Gertrude. And at that point he made a gesture that even Gertrude could understand. Alice continued the conversation, but raised a hand in horror at one point, interrupting the flow.

Finally Pierre's hands were still. They sank like tired birds, to rest between his thighs as he sat on the wall. His face was scarlet and he was sweating.

"My God," said Alice softly.

Gertrude could contain herself no longer. "I want to know what happened," she said. "Now tell me and let's have it all straight."

Just at that moment Pierre rose and walked to the far end of the garden. He put one foot up on the wall and looked out over the valley — isolated from them completely, not even watching their faces.

"What a horrid story," Alice said. "Two days ago his father had to go to Culoz to see about some legal business — their vineyard was under attack because they were slow with the interest on the mortgage, and he was trying to arrange some sort of loan — but that was the night he telephoned us and asked me to go over to his house and tell his son he'd have to stay overnight. Do you remember?"

"Yes," Gertrude said.

"Well, that was early evening, and guess who showed up when it got dark . . ."

"I can guess," said Gertrude. "I get it psychically. Debat."

"You're right," said Alice. "And he had a liter of Marc with him, that horrible green brandy."

"And he got little Pierre drunk," said Gertrude.

"Sometimes I think you really are psychic," Alice said.
"Yes, that's exactly what happened. And then they staggered out into the cornfield, and . . . and . . ."

"I can guess," said Gertrude. "I saw that one gesture, where he stuck his finger through that circle of his other fingers . . . and then pointed to his . . . er . . . behind"

"Yes," said Alice. "Except that Pierre had first given the sign for 'dishonored' and when I asked him to repeat it, that's when he became more graphic."

"And then what," asked Gertrude.

"That's about all," said Alice, "except that Grand Pierre found out about it."

"How exactly."

"I haven't the foggiest, and Pierre wouldn't say. At any rate, Grand Pierre accused Debat, and Debat sneered at him and asked him how he liked his son himself, and they had a scene about incest being even worse than buggery, and there was very bad blood between the two."

"And Grand Pierre was in the field to settle the argument, I suppose."

"I don't know," Alice said. "I suppose so."

Then both of them were silent. They looked down the garden at Petit Pierre, who had not moved.

"After that," Gertrude said finally, "I guess anything could happen."

Alice shook her head. "And maybe it did," she said darkly.

❧ VI ❧

Law'n'Order

WHEN THEY GOT TO BELLEY with P'tit Pierre, Gertrude took the car to the garage because it had something wrong with the axle.

On the way, she said, "I don't know what, it is a mystery, I hope it ain't bent from those rutty roads and all the stones we hit underneath."

They had put Petit Pierre in the back seat whilst Alice sat in the front, filing her scarlet nails, something she did whenever she was worried, bored, tired, happy, calm, sitting in her rocker, or riding in the car. With Pierre back there she could not talk to him, and besides she had nothing to say to him at the moment. Finally she turned and signed: "What is the word for — " She wanted to say "axle" but since she didn't know the French for it, she turned around, quite frustrated.

They all got out of the car in the garage, and Alice and Pierre waited while Gertrude explained things to the mechanic.

"Let's walk across the square," Gertrude said. "I love things that are round but I love squares too, you can put a circle in the square and maybe that's the way you square a circle."

"It isn't," said Alice.

The two of them were a somewhat odd-looking pair. Gertrude this day had donned a black skirt, a dark grey quilted vest with a pale pink blouse, and she stalked like a heavy-footed hunter across the square diagonally, avoiding the central tree with its circular stone border, with Alice and Pierre following behind. Alice was really the colorful one. She wore a black print silk dress, on which poppies and bright-colored flowers flamed in the air. On her wide-brimmed hat of black shiny straw was a corbeille of fruits and vegetables — huge and eye-arresting. That, with the great hump of her nose, the more-than-faint mustache, the bangs, and the purple beads looped three times around her neck and hanging to her knees, made her quite a figure. In one hand she had a beaded fringed carry-all, about a third as large as she was, for she was a small bent woman. Gertrude strode upright, like a yeoman of the guard, her grey hair combed forward and decorating her forehead.

"Do we look all right for the gendarmerie?" Alice whispered.

Of course."

Pierre walked behind them. He seemed to have improved somewhat: his stride was young and male, aggressive. His golden hair fell decently around his face, his strong brown hands swung easily by his side, his feet in his open sandals were clean, and he looked extremely confident. For look you, was he not with the *demoiselles américaines* who had interested themselves in his problem? They would find his father — soon.

They strode bravely with purpose into the gendarmerie.
"We are here," said Gertrude, "to speak with the chief
of police."

"Ah — Monsieur Gallos," said the male secretary, a
young man who looked fixedly at Pierre's middle, and then
up at Gertrude. "Monsieur the Capitaine. What is the purpose of your visit?"

"We will speak but with Capitaine Gallos," said Gertrude. "It is a matter of confidence."

"Bien entendu," said the young man. Alice could have
sworn that he made a small wink in Pierre's direction, but
perhaps it was only a tic. "Just a moment. I will see if he is
occupied. May I say who calls?"

"Gertrude Stein and friends," Gertrude announced in
her pulpit voice.

"Ah yes — les demoiselles américaines. I will inform
him at once."

He went through the door. "It pays to be famous," said
Gertrude, turning to Alice, whose fingers flickered briefly
to Pierre.

The young clerk ushered them into the office of the prefect. It was a room like all bureaucratic rooms in France:
painted dull green with a waist-high baseboard of ugly
brown. The captain sat behind a cluttered desk on which re-
posed two wire correspondence baskets and a telephone. He
was a florid man with grey hair and a fearsome mustache,
whose ends curled up toward his eyes. He rose to greet
them.

"I," said Gertrude, "am Mademoiselle Gertrude Stein
and this is my secretary Mademoiselle Alice Toklas. We ac-
company a young man, Monsieur Pierre Desjardins."

"I am honored to see the great and well-known
American writer and her friends," said Monsieur Gallos,

bowing a little at the waist. "Will you please be seated?"
There were two chairs. Gertrude and Alice sat down,
and Pierre stood.

"What is it that I may do for you?"

"We are here to report a missing person," said Gertrude.
"The father of this young man whom you perhaps know."

"Ah yes. How long has he been missing?"

"Since day before yesterday," Alice said, translating for
Pierre's benefit.

Monsieur Gallos stroked his mustache. "Is he in the
habit of absenting himself for short or long periods?"

"Never," said Gertrude.

"I perceive that Mademoiselle Toklas is making signs
with her fingers," said the chief. "Is the young man then
damaged in some fashion — the ears perhaps?"

"He is a sourd-muet," said Gertrude. "And my friend is
translating for him."

"I believe that I remember of his affliction," said
Gallos. "It is most unfortunate."

"We should like you to institute a search for his father,"
said Gertrude.

"Ah yes," said Monsieur Gallos. "That, we will do tomorrow. By law, three days must elapse before we can
begin. Meanwhile, would you be so kind as to fill out these
forms? There are six of them, and each must be filled out as
an original. No carbon paper is allowed."

"My God," said Alice in English, picking up a form and
looking at it. "This alone will take a week to do." And in
French she asked, "Why so many?"

"For the prefect, the subprefect, the canton, the com-
mune, the arrondissement, and one for the Ministry in
Paris," he said, beaming. "It is a great labor, I know, but it
has its advantages."

"What, may I ask," said Gertrude.

He stroked his mustache again. "Well, it stops a wife from running to us if her husband gets drunk and stays in Culoz overnight. Or it keeps a husband from complaining if his wife stays away from him for a day or two. It is an addition to the Napleonic code which was added by President LeBrun," he said, waving to a large picture of LeBrun on the wall, scowling beneath two draped tricolors. "And it saves us work, for after all we have only three police in our force."

Alice picked up the forms and straightened them together. "We will be happy to do it," she said. "But that will mean the murderer will have a three days' start."

"*What?!*" shouted Monsieur Gallos.

Gertrude smiled. "We will be happy to tell you as much as we know," she said, "if your clerk can take shorthand or make notes."

"And if he is confidential," Alice added. But Monsieur Gallos was already at the door. He flung it open and called, "Claude! Bring your notepad!"

"Is he trustworthy," Gertrude asked. "Can he keep a secret. For after all, what Mademoiselle Toklas and I are about to tell you should be in the strictest confidence."

"He is most discreet and dependable," said Monsieur Gallos. Then he turned to Claude who had appeared in the doorway, looking a little nervous.

"Claude," he said, frowning severely. "What you are about to hear and to make notations on is to be kept in the strictest secrecy. You are not to discuss it with anyone except myself. You understand?"

Claude nodded and sat down on a chair he brought with him.

And between them they told him the entire story, beginning with Alice seeing Desjardins running down the furrows, carrying a filet, shaking his fist at Debat. Alice's fingers flew in complex patterns for Petit Pierre's benefit, but when they came to the young man's being seduced and raped by Debat, her hands were still, folded in her lap. She was watching Claude, who shot a swift look at Pierre, and with his lips nearly closed moved the barest edge of his tongue-tip from one corner of his mouth to the other. *Ah there, Claude,* Alice thought, *we perceive a small secret of your own.*

When they finished, Monsieur Gallos looked very grave and troubled. "These are matters of great concern and seriousness," he said finally. "And we must proceed with caution, since they are so far only suspicions. I will ask for assistance from a policier, an excellent detective, whom I know in Culoz. Meanwhile, I cannot stress too much the importance of your telling no one of this affair."

"Understood, Monsieur," said Gertrude, rising. "We will tell no one, and not discuss it save amongst ourselves. And Alice will also caution young Pierre."

When they were leaving the station, Gertrude muttered, "I always thought that 'policier' meant a detective story."

"So it does," said Alice, "but to a policeman it means a detective."

"You sound like me sometimes," said Gertrude.

"We sound like each other," Alice said.

Outside in the calm sunlight of the afternoon, Alice cautioned Pierre to say nothing to anyone about the affair. "You promise not to talk about it?" she signed to him.

"Yes," he said.

Then Alice turned to Gertrude and said in English, "Shall I warn him about Claude's reaction?"

"What reaction," Gertrude said.

"I think that Claude wants Pierre."

Gertrude shook her head. "Whatever happens in that case," she said, "is certainly no affair of ours, and if the two of them want to play at two-backed beast, let us not throw stones."

"Perish forbid," said Alice. "Our own glass house might break."

❦ VII ❦

Johnny-Jump-Up

A WHOLE WEEK WENT BY and nothing happened.

Gertrude went into the garden that morning and found Alice at her endless task of snipping dead leaves from the flower-plots.

"Isn't this the day that Petit Pierre comes," she demanded.

"Yes, but so far there's been no word from him," Alice said. "I'll have to run over to his house and see about him. He'll have to get here so I can let him through the gate. Before we leave for Culoz to collect Johnny-jump-up."

Gertrude laughed. "I forget why we ever began to call him that," she said.

"Last year when he was here," Alice said. "Don't you remember? He was always jumping up to help do something — take out the plates when we were perfectly capable of it, or to light my cigarette, or to move a chair out of the sun or into it, a regular jumping-jack."

"Oh yes," said Gertrude, and then, "why is it Pussy that

there has been no word from Monsieur Gallos the police chief nor any word from anybody, that is very puzzling, more of a mystery than the real mystery."

"Oh, there's been plenty of talk," Alice said, trying to shake a dewy leaf loose from her glove. "All the families in Bilignin are a-buzz, and they've all been asking P'tit Pierre questions, lots of them, writing scads of notes to him about it and he to them, and I guess he's still worried sick about it all."

"Maybe Johnny will be able to help," Gertrude said. "Do you remember how after he left last year he wrote a two-page letter about — well, he called it a detective story and it was very hard to figger out, except you did, you found the answer in the room he'd been sleeping in."

Alice shrugged. "It was simple. The old wallpaper still up there had that medallion pattern, and I just followed the directions since he wrote them in your style, and finally found the medallion in which he had written in pencil the words 'I love Gertrude and Alice more than anything and always will.' "

Gertrude laughed. "Yes, that was nice, very nice, and he took my palm-print and then left some books behind in the secret cupboard, Henry Miller's *Tropic of* something-or-other as I think, but then I don't very much like Henry Miller, he's too vulgar."

"We must remember to give those books back to him this time," Alice said.

"But I am a little worried about Johnny," Gertrude said. "Do you think we will be able to control him now do you."

"Yes," Alice said. "He's young, well fairly so, won't he be twenty-seven this year, and he's inclined to whoring, but he's also very much in awe of you and if you frown at him he will leave the boys of Belley alone."

"I wonder if he'll be able to help us with the mystery, what do you think."

"He may," said Alice. "He's got a keen mind and he reads detective stories almost as much as you do. He can do the footwork for us, the running around."

"Yes," said Gertrude. "I think we might as well start to look for Monsieur Desjardins ourselves, the police seem very lackadaisical, and after all we have been able to find out things before and probably will again."

"Of course we will," Alice said, patting Gertrude on the shoulder. "I'll go right now and get Petit Pierre, and then we'll leave for Culoz."

She was gone about ten minutes and returned with the young man, who looked even more pale and wan than before.

"Oh what can ail thee, knight-at-arms," Gertrude murmured when she saw him.

"He does look a bit pale beneath all that tan," said Alice. "And he has heard nothing. The police came to interview him — with pad and pencil — but he could tell them nothing we had not told Monsieur Gallos."

Gertrude extended her hand to Pierre, who shook it briefly and smiled with a small nod of his head.

"Take up all the weeds in the flower plots today," Alice signed to Pierre, "and rake the leaves by the main gate. We are going to Culoz and will be back late this afternoon."

She also spoke aloud as her fingers moved, so that Gertrude could hear. "And you know how to unlock the front gate," she said, "so you can go home when you have finished."

"I have nothing else to do," Pierre said. "Will it be all right if I sit in the sun in the lounge chair until you return? To become a little bronzé?"

"Of course," said Alice. "And if you get thirsty Chen will make you a citron pressé ... But if he gets any more bronzé," said Alice to Gertrude, "we'll have to get a pedestal for him."

Then there was the usual flurry as they got ready to leave in the Matford, with the two dogs yapping and raising hell because they could not go along. Basket, the huge white poodle, stood on his hind legs and pawed the air about a foot above Gertrude's head, and Pepe, the chihuahua, yipped so shrilly that each bark raised his tiny body well off the ground.

"No no boys," Gertrude said, "you can't go this time, you must stay home and protect the house and bark at the burglars. And you, Basket," she said, sternly addressing the poodle, "Be fierce. Play Hemingway."

The black Matford roared away. Gertrude's driving was an awesome thing. She would affix herself firmly to the seat with its extra cushion, arrange the padding behind her back, let her shoulders sink and round forward whilst clutching the steering wheel as if it were a life preserver. Her whole expression changed, from that of a smiling Buddha to a scowling avenger — brows drawn down, eyes narrowed almost to slits, and a vein throbbing in her forehead. Then she would step on the starter and off they would go, raising great clouds of dust and scattering squawking chickens whilst the peasants would scramble to safety at the side of the road. She was never really very happy until the speedometer registered one hundred — kilometers, not miles — per hour. Then she felt burly and dominant and sea-shouldering, like Keat's whale. She loved the sense of power, and Alice had long since ceased to remonstrate with her, beyond remarking occasionally that each twenty miles of Lovey's driving gave her one more grey hair. An afternoon's driving would sometimes add at least five or six new ones.

The drive to Culoz was not a long one, and the sturdy Matford pulled up at the station about fifteen minutes before the rapido was due from Paris. Gertrude stalked back and forth on the platform, peered at a crate of muttering chickens, adjusted her waistband, smoothed her hair, and was finally reduced to sitting on the bench alongside Alice — who was still filing her nails.

"I hate meeting trains and saying goodbye to them and I hate waiting for them especially."

"Be calm, Lovey," said Alice. "I hear the rails beginning to sing."

"I don't hear a thing," said Gertrude.

Alice sighed and tucked her nail-file into her reticule. "Alas," she said, "they say the hearing is the first thing to go."

Gertrude frowned. "Not so," she said. "It's taste." And she looked at Alice, whose turn it then was to frown.

But they were both smiling as the train huffed into the station.

❧ VIII ❧

Touch-Me-Not

WHAT A REUNION!

Hugs and kisses on cheeks, and pattings, and mild shrieks of laughter, and chuckles — euphoria and brilliant storms of talk, talk, talk!

Johnny threw his suitcase into the rear seat, and followed it with his longish legs and body. He was a lean sort of person with brownish hair and a darker mustache, which he wore mainly because no one else was wearing liphair at that time. He was, alas, a somewhat respected professor at some Chicago university named after a saint [although Gertrude often confused the name of it with a dog's paw], but he was more or less a whore at night, or a hunter of stags, or some kind of predator. His middle initial was "A" which actually stood for Actaeon, although he never told that to anyone. Thus, his initials spelled *jam*, and he was proud of that gift of butch from his parents. Like Actaeon, he had come upon Artemis-Gertrude naked in the bathroom the year before, and had been changed, although dogs had not torn him to pieces, nor had she. It was he who kept Alice sup-

47

plied with kitchen gadgets, and sent bundles of paperback
detective stories to Gertrude. They loved him for various
reasons, none of them the least sexual.

"Do we ever have something to tell you," Gertrude
flung at him over her shoulder as they drove back to
Bilignin. "There is a mystery afoot."

"Deep, dark, and horrid," said Alice.

"A man has disappeared, a farmer and a neighbor —"
Gertrude began.

"— who has a son, a beauty if there ever were one, a
sourd-muet . . ." and so the story rolled away, in a kind of
antiphonal chant for two alternating voices, the magnificent contralto of Gertrude followed by the huskier baritone
of Alice. And so the Greek play, with chorus responding,
went on and on, the words carried by the rushing wind from
front to rear, and out the window — words that Johnny
heard as in a tranquil reverie, for the fragrant air and the late
September heat combined with his Pernod hangover to put
him almost into the arms of Somnus, from which state he
was suddenly jolted awake as he heard the hair-raising story
of the harvesting of Petit Pierre's *pucelage*.

"Er. . ." he said, "this so handsome young man — a
deaf-mute, you say?"

The choral flow of the Greek play was interrupted. "He
is that," said Gertrude, "and it annoys me that Alice is the
only one who can finger-talk with him . . . unless you can."
And here she went against her habit, and used a rising inflection.

"It so happens," said Johnny-jump-up, "that I can. I
knew a fellow once . . . " and his voice turned dreamy.
What the deaf lacked in ears, they made up for in so many
other ways . . .

"Good, good," Alice interrupted. "My fingers grow mighty tired sometimes. Now you can help."

"That leaves me more out in the cold than ever," Gertrude grumbled.

"Not so," said Alice. "Now you'll have two interpreters to make sure you hear everything, right down to semicolons and commas. And we can correct each other and find synonyms — in short, do all your copyediting for you, discover cognates in foreign tongues, explain early forms even from Anglo-Saxon and Middle English. We will be your double encyclopedia."

"That will certainly tell me more than I want to know," said Gertrude, "and all that will stop me from listening and certainly from ever writing another word."

"We'll see," said Alice.

But still the talk, the air, the pleasant poplars lining the road, the sweet odors of new-mown hay and the fragrance of the vineyards — all of it made Johnny's eyes keep slipping half-shut, and then opening wide as he struggled to absorb the charms of the day and the talk. How dreadful, he thought, to fall asleep when you have finally arrived once again at Bilignin and are in the lustrous company of the pair who fascinate you most.

They stopped at the massive iron gate to the château, and he sprang from the backseat to open the gate and lift his luggage from the car. The dogs greeted them with great barkings and leapings, and Chen came running.

"And who is that?" asked Johnny in English, as the young Indochine struggled manfully with the luggage.

"Chen," said Alice. "He attends the Sorbonne, is wretchedly poor, and we have brought him down as houseboy, so that he wouldn't starve this summer. He is young and quite elegant. I believe his father is a prince or something, deposed from his throne."

As they rounded the house to go into the garden they came upon Petit Pierre, stretched out nearly naked in the lounge chair, his ankles crossed, his magnificent thighs and torso gleaming with sweat. He was wearing only the tiniest black nylon *slip,* his shirt and blue trousers lying on the ground beside him.

"Good God," said Johnny, stopping in his tracks.

"What's wrong," asked Gertrude.

He shook his head. "I am struck dumb by beauty. Look at those lovely muscles. I have fallen in love for the four hundred and eleventh time since arriving three weeks ago in France."

"It will pass," said Alice. "He is cut off from the world. That is P'tit Pierre."

"The deaf-mute?"

"The same," said Gertrude. "See — he is asleep, he did not hear us arrive, you must touch him if you want to waken him."

"Not I," said Johnny. "I feel like Euclid looking on beauty bare."

"Go ahead," said Alice. "And then sign to him a bonjour."

With a sigh, Johnny touched the naked shoulder. Pierre's eyes flew open, and an astonishing thing happened. With a kind of combined subhuman growl and screech, Pierre sprang to his feet, eyes glazed and unseeing, and his face contorted into a mask of rage and hatred. He lunged at Johnny who quickly stepped back, as did Gertrude and Alice, forming a kind of half-circle with Pierre in the center.

Alice's fingers flickered. "He is a friend," she signed.

Pierre's face crumpled, and his eyes slowly returned to

their brilliant blue. And then his fingers themselves seemed to be stuttering, nervous. And then without warning he burst suddenly into tears, making no sounds at all, but crying.

Gertrude approached him and patted his shoulder. His silent sobbing continued for a moment, and then he raised his head and looked at them. His cheeks were wet, and diamonds spilled from his eyes.

"I am sorry, really," his fingers said again. "I was dreaming . . . I thought I was being attacked."

"Ah," said Gertrude.

Alice signed an introduction, finger-spelling Johnny's last name by the letters. Pierre advanced a step and shook hands with him.

And all seemed well. But Alice signed no more. She seemed to be deep in thought.

✿ IX ✿

An Odyssey of Sorts

"Now looky here," Gertrude commanded in a loud voice, stepping out of the living room into the garden. There were some sheets of blue paper in her hands, with typing on them.

Johnny opened a languid eye, scarcely recovered from the monumental binge of his preceding days in Paris, and looked up at her from the lounge chair.

"Yes, m'dear," he said. "What's up?"

"Well, I see you are but barely," said Gertrude, noticing the pale lavender under his eyes. "Did you sleep well and are you recovered, Pernod will get you quicker than anything and stay with you longer."

"How did you know it was Pernod?" asked Johnny, blushing.

"You smelled as if you'd fallen into the lickerish barrel," Gertrude said. "I mean licorice, I always pronounce them the same."

"It was both barrels," said Johnny. "Lickerish and lico-rice. Or maybe you could even combine the two, lust and anise, and come up with liquorish."

"Whatever," said Gertrude. "Either or both." She waved the papers at him. "See these."

"What do you have there?" Johnny asked.

"Questions," Gertrude said. "Alice and I made them up this morning and she typed them. We are going to take them into Belley, into all the stores and ask if they remember Grand Pierre being there and when and did he buy anything, so it will be an odyssey of discovery and exploration."

"Don't you suppose the police have already done that?" Johnny asked.

"I suppose they have if they're on their toes, but who knows, I want to know myself and so does Alice and we'll never know what they know unless we nose it out ourselves, now will we."

Johnny had to listen very carefully, but he followed her perfectly.

"We all want to nose," he said with a grin.

She thrust a sheet of paper at him. On it in neat lines down the page was a number of questions:

Do you know Monsieur Pierre Desjardins, called in the region by the nickname of Grand Pierre?

Was he in your store a week ago last Monday?

If so, what time of day?

If so, did he buy anything?

What did he buy?

If he bought anything, did he take it with him?

In a bag or what?

Was he alone?

Has anyone from the gendarmerie been in your
store to ask you these questions?

If so, when?

Have you by any chance seen M. Desjardins
since then?

Thank you very much. Que vous êtes tout à fait
aimable.

And below the questions in Alice's tiny thin spidery handwriting, done with her miniscule Spenserian nib, was a list
of shops:

La Quincaillerie Exquise

Le Tabac Mondial

La Fruiterie d'Ain

Le Bistro des Deux Éléphants

"Heavens above," said Johnny, looking at the name of
his first stop. "Do you mean to say there's a shop called The
Exquisite Hardware Store?"

"Indeed there is," said Gertrude. "It's got all kinds of
junk in it from posy seeds to pepper-mills, moulins à
poivre. And Alice and I will divide up the other eight stores.
She's going to go to the laiterie, the milk and cheese place,
the charcuterie the butcher, the tailleur and the pressing,
and the usine where they make noodles. And I will go to the
other bistro, Le Cygne Mourant The Dying Swan, the
bakery La Grande Boulangerie, the grocery L'Épicerie de
Brillat-Savarin, the shoe-shop La Chaussure Élégant. And
then in a half-hour we will all meet at the department store
Le Grand Magasin d'Ain."

"Such fancy names for a small town," Johnny murmured, smoothing his mustache with the back of his fore-finger. "Sounds like the Place Vendôme in Paris."

"The smaller the place the bigger the name," said Gertrude. "Now do you understand everything. And by the way, at the tabac get Alice some cigarettes, some Baltos, she said, provided they don't have any American cigarettes and if they do get Dunhills if they've got 'em but she doesn't think they do. Now are you sure about everything."

"Yes," Johnny said, "except what's the French for nickname?"

"Ask Alice," said Gertrude. "Come on, let's go, she has already unlocked the gate. And take notes, will you. Do you have a pencil."

"Yes," he said, unfolding himself from the lounge chair. Gertrude got up from the stone garden wall and with one hand absently brushed the dust from her ample bottom.

Alice had opened the gate and was standing beside the Matford. "Did you tell Johnny everything?" she asked.

"Even about your cigarettes," said Gertrude.

They all climbed into the Matford, with Johnny in the back seat. Alice got her nail file out of her bag.

"What's the French word for nickname?" Johnny asked her.

"Use 'sobriquet'," said Alice. And to Gertrude, "Now Lovey, drive slow. We are in no great hurry."

Gertrude settled herself on her favorite cushion and pulled at the one behind her back. "All right, all right," she said. Then she gave two horrendous blasts on the horn. Chen came running from the house.

"Fermez la grille," Gertrude shouted at him.

"S'il vout plaît!" Alice yelled. Basket and Pepe shattered the morning air with barkings.

Gertrude gunned the Matford, throwing all of them

hard back against their seats. The car shot out of the driveway, narrowly missing one of Mademoiselle Delarue's chickens, which with wild cacklings flew upward and bounced off the right fender of the car. Behind them Chen shut the iron gate with a clang that rattled the air.

"Good fathers," said Alice, "we'll all be killed."

"Nonsense," said Gertrude. "I'm a fine driver and I know the way."

"Considering that there are no branchings from here to Belley, that's no great accomplishment," said Alice with a muffled snort.

"There is too a branching," said Gertrude, hunched over the wheel. "It goes to the caserne where all the Sénégalese soldiers are, don't you remember."

"We may need a few to haul us out of the ditch," said Alice.

In the backseat Johnny was silently practicing what he remembered of the Our Father in Anglo-Saxon. It always had a calming effect on him, but he could never remember past *Urne gedaeghwamlican hlaf syle us to daeg.*

❧ X ❧

Successes Here and There

JOHNNY FINISHED HIS TOUR of the four places in exactly twenty minutes. He looked around the little town square of Belley, located the the Grand Magasin d'Ain — right next to the Hôtel Pernollet — and then returned for a quick one to Le Bistro des Deux Éléphants. He gulped down the small glass of cheap brandy and went out into the square again, thoughtfully dissolving on his tongue one of the highly perfumed Pearls of the Pyrenées that he had found in the tobacco store, remembering that their violet color [and taste!], containing a drop of sarcanthus scent — the true essence of the male crystallized in a piece of sugar — had been adored by Huysmans in *À Rebours*, the book that had so fascinated Oscar Wilde. The strong and piercing fumes, released from the hoar-front of sugar, entered his tongue with almost unendurable strength, reminding him of waters opalescent with rare liqueurs, and deep searching kisses, fragrant with the overwhelming odors that mounted to his brain and called up memories of the nakedness and savor of certain men.

"Wow!" he said to himself. "At least Gertrude won't be able to smell the brandy." For despite her great tolerance of all the weaknesses and foibles of the human spirit, she found it difficult as she grew older to put up with all the tumult and the shouting that originated in the drunken mind. And Johnny seldom dared take more than a sip of wine at dinner while in her presence. The bottle of Courvoisier that he had brought with him in his suitcase was for emergencies only.

Alice was already in the tiny store of the Grand Magasin. She was at the sewing counter looking at some red silk thread, and from a fresh-faced country girl had just purchased a spool.

"I have always found," she said to Johnny, "that when I have to baste small stitches in sheets and pillowcases, it's a lot easier to use red thread. You can never find the white on white."

Just then Gertrude entered the door and saw them. She approached, waving her sheet of paper.

"And what did you all find," she asked.

"We will have to have a conference," said Alice. "Let us go into the square and sit on one of the benches under a tree."

And all three marched out, with Gertrude's stocky figure parting the waves and Alice following behind her, and the lean and muscular figure of Johnny-jump-up coming along at the rear.

They sat down on a wooden bench under a poplar tree in the middle of the square. A few lackadaisical pigeons watched them approach, and then went on with their aimless pecking.

"Now Johnny, what did you find," Gertrude asked.

"Well, they remembered him at the Exquisite Hardware," he said, referring to his sheet of paper. "He was the first customer of the day when they opened at nine o'clock. He bought a small paint brush, a tenth of a kilo of coquelicot seeds, spokes for a bicycle wheel, a small paring knife with a serrated edge to cut tomatoes and things, and a half-kilo of small nails — galvanized roofing nails from what the woman showed me. Incidentally, she was terrible — a regular shrew and she looked like a medieval witch. Her nose and chin almost touched, and I think all her teeth were gone."

"That was Mademoiselle Guerre," said Gertrude. "We don't get along at all which is why we sent you to the Exquisite Hardware store instead of us, she wouldn't have spoken to us at all."

"Did you ask about the police, Johnny?" Alice said.

"Yes, and they had been there last week. The woman said it was a strange policeman named Duvalle, and she had never seen him in the town before."

"That must have been the detective from Culoz," Gertrude said.

"I guess they really are beginning to take it seriously," Alice added.

Johnny looked at his list again. "At the tabac he bought some Gitanes and a small box of tabac prisé — snuff, I guess that is. At about nine-fifteen, but the man couldn't remember exactly. He was grumpy. Said he had already told the police everything. And here," he said to Alice, "are your Baltos."

She started digging in her carry-all. "How much are they?"

"Never mind," said Johnny. "From me to you. And then

I went to the Fruiterie d'Ain. He hadn't been there at all, at least so the young clerk said. The propriétaire was not there at the moment so I couldn't ask about the police."

"Good, good," said Gertrude. "You'll make a detective yet."

"I already have . . . several," Johnny murmured, but since he was not on the side of Gertrude's good ear, she didn't hear him. But Alice did, and smiled.

At that moment Alice nudged Gertrude. "Look," she said. "Isn't that the young Claude who is the secretary to Monsieur Gallos of the police?"

Gertrude squinted at him. "It is that," she said.

The young man was crossing the square, headed in the direction of The Dying Swan. He wore a well-cut blue suit and had a red scarf tied around his neck. His left forearm was bent at the elbow and carried parallel to the ground; from the end of it his hand drooped downward and swung gently on a somewhat loose wrist. He carried his head high, and his eyes darted in all directions.

"Four hundred and twelve times," Johnny murmured to himself.

"I have a splendid idea," Alice said.

"Wot's that," said Gertrude.

Alice turned to Johnny. "How would you like to play Mata Hari?"

He sighed. "I'm really not at my best in chiffon veils," he said.

Alice laughed. "It won't be painful at all," she said. "You see, we can't learn much from the police about the disappearance of Grand Pierre, but there's always the possibility that someone might pick up some information from that young man. It might entail dreadful sacrifices, of course, and take you to a strange bed."

"How awful," said Johnny.

Gertrude laughed. "But think of the wonderful rewards," she said. "We would know what the police had found out and what their next moves were going to be, and know everything as soon as they did or sooner."

"It would involve undercover work," Alice said with a straight face.

Johnny giggled. "I'll say it would," he said.

"Then go," said Gertrude, giving him a gentle push. "He's going into the Dying Swan for a drink, go ahead and join him, you're an American, a stranger in the Bugey, be glamorous, buy him a brandy."

Johnny took off. He walked with an easy swinging stride.

"Into the jaws of death," Alice murmured.

"Hardly that," said Gertrude. "But I get it in a queer kind of way he's going to get what he goes for. Now what did you find out."

"Grand Pierre was in the laiterie at about nine-thirty," Alice said, peering at her paper. "He bought a half kilo of camembert, some butter, and some cheap cheese of the district. Then he went to the usine for noodles, nouilles, and bought some of what passes for spaghetti in these parts. That's all. What did you discover?"

"He did not have a drink in the bistro," said Gertrude, "but he bought a small baguette in the bakery. He was not in the shoe-shop, and although he went into the grocery he bought nothing."

"So," said Alice. "It was a usual trip for him. He could have carried it all in a filet."

"And he did," said Gertrude. "The woman in the épicerie noticed him and looked him over carefully when he left without buying anything, but since he had all his purchases in a filet she could see that he hadn't stolen anything from the grocery."

"Perish forbid," said Alice. "Not that he would have. He was always an honest man."

Gertrude looked troubled. "You've used the past tense," she said.

"I know," said Alice. "I am afraid that's what we'll use from now on about him."

With that sombre thought they sat silent for a few minutes. A leaf or two drifted down from the poplar. Gertrude sighed.

"The summer is almost over," she said. "We must soon be thinking about going back to Paris. Somehow in a funny kind of way I wish Francis and Cecil wouldn't be coming to visit. That Cecil. What a dumb thing to do, that advertisement with the tiny print. Tiny print always makes everyone get out their magnifying glass. They say it was worse against the Jews than the Protocols of Zion."

"Or Céline's trash," said Alice. "Two awful men." She turned sidewise on the bench to face Gertrude. "I can always send a telegram to Francis telling him we are indisposed."

"We'll think about it," said Gertrude. "I am rather tired of him too."

"Thornton said he never concealed from you his dislike of Francis."

"You should have heard Thornie carry on," Gertrude said, chuckling. "He called Francis a semi-simian baronet making disgusting toothy attempts at prettiness, and faking a little lost-boy pathos but really drenched in aggressive selfishness."

Alice giggled. "Thornie really has a way with words."

At that moment Gertrude looked across the square.

Johnny and Claude came out of the bar. "Johnny is a rather handsome young man," she said.

"He's got muscles," Alice said. "He's quite an ornament in the rose-garden while he's sunbathing. But he's scared to death of you."

"Phoo," Gertrude said. "I think he's scareder of you."

"Look at them," Alice said. "I'll wager they've made a date. Johnny has his arm around Claude's shoulders."

"Now maybe we'll really begin to find out things," Gertrude said.

Alice sniffed a little. "On top of what we already know," she said, "from just looking at them."

❧ XI ❧

The Snows of Yesteryear

ALICE, DUSTING IN THE LIVING ROOM, found a yellowed piece of paper behind the rack of the small rosewood clavichord, which was never opened. Gertrude did not like music but sometimes ran her fingers over the black keys, never the white ones.

She unfolded the paper.

"Good heavens," she said. It was an ancient program of a Saturday string orchestra class recital at the Sherman Clay Music Hall in San Francisco. Thursday. April 25th, 1901. 8:30 p.m.. "With the co-operation of Miss Alice B. Toklas."

"How well I remember," she mused. "But I've forgotten what I played."

Inside the program, she saw that she had performed Beethohen's "Adagio" from the *Pathétique*, Shubert's "Scherzo" and "Fugato" from the *Fantaisie*, and Bach's "Prelude and Fugue in B minor."

She lifted the lid to the keys of the small clavichord and looked somewhat wistfully at their yellowed ivory.

"Such a pity," she sighed. "I might have been great. I have grown old in love and I am still in love with loving. And Lovey."

... who at that very moment appeared in the doorway.

"Has Johnny jumped up yet," she demanded.

"I haven't heard him, Lovey," said Alice. "And I am done with dusting. I'll go up and waken him."

"I wonder what happened," said Gertrude.

"The usual, I suppose."

"Do you suppose he wormed anything out of that young Claude," asked Gertrude.

"I think 'wormed' is hardly the right verb," said Alice, "but we shall hear shortly." She left the room to call him.

Soon Johnny descended the stairs, wearing a light maroon pullover and a pair of grey slacks. He was limping a little. Alice followed him into the living room.

"Good morning," said Gertrude. "You are limping. What happened."

"For all his ladylike ways," said Johnny, "that is a very strong young man, with great talents in wrestling. My ankle was twisted when he took hold of it to turn me over on my stomach."

"Spare us," said Alice, frowning a little. "Did you discover anything?"

"Well, yes and no. He was reluctant to talk at first. Then I told him that I was visiting you and knew all about everything anyway. I told him of our little expedition yesterday and what we had learned. But he knew all of that already, for he had gone with the policier Duvalle on the same kind of expedition a few days ago."

"Do they have any clues about Grand Pierre's whereabouts," asked Gertrude.

"Not a one."

"What about Debat, do they suspect him."

"That's where the yes and no come in," said Johnny. "He said the capitaine believes that Alice saw Grand Pierre and Debat in the field on that Monday morning, but the fact that Alice alone witnessed it and saw no fight of any kind creates a very delicate situation. They are going to question Debat later today — and tell him that he was seen in the field with Desjardins, but they are not going to tell him who saw him. It would seem that no one can make a complaint against Debat because nothing was seen to happen. And he cannot be held on mere suspicion. They will have to find something tangible, something concrete, before they can make any charges about anything. And nothing seems to be turning up. *Corpus delicti.* The body is missing."

"How is Petit Pierre," Gertrude asked.

"All right, I guess. Duvalle could speak to him in signs, a little. I think he discovered that P'tit Pierre hated his father."

"He was very strict with him," said Alice. "I mean, he always has been. Wrong tense again," she added.

"So far," said Gertrude. "But then everyone hates Debat."

"What has that to do with it?" Alice asked. "Debat is still here. It is Grand Pierre who has vanished."

"Then," said Johnny, "there is one more point, and that is still more delicate. Claude said that if anything is found — anything tangible, such as a dead body — then Alice's testimony will be terribly important. And *that* means also that Alice — to use his words — will be placed *aux grands risques et périls.* At great risks and perils. Hasard. From Debat. She might have to be taken into 'protective custody'."

"Good fathers," said Alice. "Would I be put in jail?"

"Perhaps," said Johnny. "Or perhaps they would station

a policeman at the gate. Or put a pistol-packin' mama in the château."

Gertrude laughed. "Don't worry Pussy, I'll come to visit you every Thursday."

"And of course you would have to testify at the trial," said Johnny. "Which might mean you'd have to come back down here in the dead of winter from Paris."

"I wish I'd never seen that damned spyglass," said Alice. "I am beginning to be terrified."

"There, there," said Gertrude. "Never mind. I get it psychically that no one is ever going to find anything. He has gone to join the Foreign Legion. Of course I am always wrong about all my hunches. I never thought for a minute the King of England would abdicate over that Simpson woman. I never thought Roosevelt would get elected a second time. And so I get it that Grand Pierre certainly has not been murdered."

"Which means," said Alice, "that he probably *has* been, since you say you're always wrong."

"Let us go have some tea why don't we" said Gertrude.

They went into the kitchen. Alice said she'd join them in a moment, and stayed in the living room. She picked up the old program of her recital.

"Perhaps," she said to herself as she tucked it out of sight behind the rack of the clavichord. "Perhaps I should have practiced harder on the piano."

But then she thought of the wonderful times since meeting Gertrude all those years ago [was it really nearly thirty-five?] and she went smiling to join them in the kitchen.

❧ XII ❧

Poor Claude

TWO DAYS PASSED, lazy ones for all of them. Alice worked around the kitchen and the house. Gertrude and Johnny took walks — in the mornings up the hill through the Desjardins' vineyards, where at one far end of the lines they glimpsed P'tit Pierre working, and in the afternoons down toward the river in the Ain valley. Gertrude hardly ever stopped talking — about Literature, Life, Wallis Simpson, the Comtes d'Aiguy, Bravig Imbs, the Baronne Pierlot, Virgil Thomson, Carl Van Vechton, Thornton Wilder, Juan Gris, Picasso, Picabia, Madame Roux, Donna Denton, Bernard Fay, and dozens more. Johnny's head swam with the names and anecdotes and judgments and pronunciamentos. But most of all she spoke long and lovingly of Basket, the huge white caniche, the white poodle that as a puppy had leaped into Gertrude's arms, and Alice had hoped would learn to carry a basket of flowers in his mouth — but alas, he never did. And she was likewise very fond of Pepe, the lecherous little chihuahua which Picabia had given her, who loved to chase chickens and eat cheese — any kind of cheese, no matter what, and could smell it a mile away and beg for it incessantly.

At four o'clock on the second afternoon Gertrude and he got back to the château, puffing as usual from the climb up the hill. Gertrude's cheeks were faintly purple.

"Are you going to have some sun," she said, as they rounded the house to the garden.

"Too late, I think," Johnny said. "I believe I'll take the bicycle and go in to Belley for some cigarettes."

"How long did you rent it for," Gertrude asked.

"It rents by the week," said Johnny.

"I'll see if Alice wants anything," said Gertrude and raised her voice. "Pussy. Oh Pussy."

Alice stuck her head around the edge of the kitchen door. "What's cooking?" she asked.

"That should be my question," said Gertrude. "Johnny's taking the bicyclette into Belley for cigarettes, do you want some, or anything at all from the stores."

"Yes," said Alice. "Stop at the épicerie and get me a small packet of saffron," she said. "Please. I want it for the rice for dinner. When will you be back? We'll eat about seven-thirty."

"Long before then, probably," said Johnny.

He wheeled the bicycle from the shed and straddled it, his legs long enough to reach the ground below the pedals. He carefully shut the gate after himself, and glided down the small incline to the road to Belley.

To tell the truth, he was a little glad to get away for a while. He needed a breath of air, and a chance to let his brain stop whirling, for Gertrude's talk and his answers kept him in a continual state of alertness. And exhaustion.

But that was the obvious surface reason, wasn't it? The

real truth was that his middle was calling. And since he had spent some very pleasant moments in Claude Oria's little house on the edge of town, he thought he might just possibly pay him another visit. For Claude was finished with his day's work at four-thirty — and would be home, probably, by the time Johnny had stopped for the saffron and the cigarettes. On this occasion he would certainly not give Claude another chance at his ankle.

It was a small white cottage with a bright green shingled roof, a tiny flower garden in front, and to one side an old-fashioned water-well with a bucket hanging from the roller. He dismounted and wheeled the bicycle into the yard, leaning it against the porch.

He heard the bell ring inside. And then there were a few sounds, as of someone painfully shuffling. "Un moment — je viens!" he heard Claude call out.

The door opened.

Alas, what was this apparition before him? For Claude was leaning heavily on one crutch. There was a bandage around his head covering one eye, and the other eye was black and blue, with faint tinges of yellow and red far down on his cheek. He wore a black and silver dressing gown.

"Au nom de Dieu!" said Johnny. "Claude — what has happened?"

"Enter," said Claude through a puffed lip. "And I will tell you."

"You look as if you have had an accident," said Johnny. "Or two accidents. Or three."

"It was not so much an accident as a misjudgment," said Claude, easing himself with great pain into a rocking chair.

"We have all made them," said Johnny sympathetically. "What was yours?"

"I was amorous," said Claude.

"A condition afflicting everyone from time to time," said Johnny, "but usually not with such sad results."

"Well, I saw that young man, Pierre Desjardins, in the square last evening, and I asked him to come for a glass of wine at the Two Éléphants . . . "

"Do you know the − ?" and Johnny could not think of the French term for sign-language, so he improvised " − the language of the fingers?"

"Ah, no," said Claude, "but love has other means of speaking. I pointed to the bistro, I made the mime of drinking and indicated I would pay. And he came with me. We had a glass or two and then we went for a walk, out toward the fields. It was a lovely evening . . . "

" . . . on such a night," murmured Johnny, remembering the line from Shakespeare.

"Yes. It was pleasant, walking in silence. Naturally we said nothing. And when we got into the field I made a sign that we should sit down. Unfortunately, when I had looked at his trousers I was convinced that the gifts which nature had bestowed on him behind his braguette had grown larger than a mere promenade among the grasses warranted, and I reached to feel if I were right . . . "

"Oh, oh!" said Johnny.

"The earth shook, the sky trembled, his fist hit my eye, he pushed me backward. I fell, he kicked me in the head and then the stomach and then my hip. I got up and he hit me again and again. I got my arms around his waist, he kneed me in the groin and hit me again. And that was the last I knew. When I recovered I was looking up at the stars and the grass was wet with dew."

"What horror!"

"Yes, I am sore all over and I am sadly out of commission. My walnuts are swollen to the size of hen's eggs. And I ache. I suffer."

"Is there anything I can do to help?"

Claude smiled wanly. "Non, merci," he said. "I will recover. But I will stay far away from your Petit Pierre."

"Not mine," said Johnny. "I will call on you again when you are recovered."

"I will be enchanted to see you again," said Claude.

On the bicycle back to Belley and through it on to Bilignin, Johnny considered the whole affair. There was a demon chained in Petit Pierre, that was quite obvious. What had caused it? The rape in the cornfield by old Debat? Something earlier in his life? His father's harsh discipline? In the silent ones (but is not everyone silent?), who can tell what Iagoan plots romp in the grey valleys of the brain? What hawks fly?

Beauty such as Pierre's should be shared. He was only temporary custodian of it. But evidently that was not the way Pierre felt about it.

He was nearly back to Bilignin when he remembered that he had left the saffron at Claude's cottage. He turned and pedaled back to Belley and bought some more at the épicerie. And then to calm his nerves he had two *fines* at the Dying Swan.

And two more Pearls of the Pyrénées, so that Gertrude wouldn't scold.

❧ XIII ❧

Season of Mists

"WHAT SHALL WE DO ABOUT Francis and Cecil," asked Gertrude, daring once again to venture into the kitchen. Chen looked up with almond eyes from his task of polishing the copper bottom of a pan, and Alice paused, a whisk in her hand above a bowl on the table. The day was grey and there was a light drizzle in the air.

"I've taken it upon myself," Alice said. "I sent them a wire and said that we were intending to leave earlier this year, and would it be all right if we saw them in Paris instead of here."

"Somehow you seem sometimes to beat me to the punch," said Gertrude. "I was just going to ask you to do that very thing and now you've done it and I am relieved and pleased both at the same time."

"And Johnny will be leaving next Tuesday," Alice said. "I tried to get him to stay over to help with the packing, but he is sailing on the Île de France on Friday and his reservation is all made, so he does have to go. But Chen will still be

73

here and that's enough. We don't have as much to carry back this year as we usually do. Mainly because I didn't do any canning this time."

"How will we ever get all the stuff and the dogs and Chen into the back seat," Gertrude asked.

"We will send Chen back on the rapido from Marseilles," said practical Alice. "It will be much simpler that way."

"What a strange story it was that Johnny told us last night," said Gertrude. "About Petit Pierre and Claude what's-his-name."

"It was strange all right," said Alice, "but hardly unexpected or unbelievable. Do you remember Pierre's reaction when he was sleeping in the sunchair and Johnny touched him on the shoulder?"

"Yes I do," said Gertrude. "It was scary but then considering what he had gone through perhaps it was if not to be expected then excused."

"I wonder if he is really the victim," Alice mused. She gave a few resounding whacks with the whisk on the edge of the bowl, to shake off the droplets of egg and batter.

"What else would he be."

"I'm not sure," said Alice. "Could he be a manipulator?"

"Bosh," said Gertrude. "The poor young man is still naïf and unsophisticated, and as for being a Machiavelli or a Borgia or a Hemingway, it's not possible, you have to be a lot older for that and a schemer and have come up against the wicked ways of the world."

"If he were by chance an idiot savant he could think of a lot of things," said Alice. "And how do we know what goes on in the head of a sourd-muet, cut off as he is from hearing and speaking? He has time to think of lots of things."

"He is neither an idiot or a savant, either separately or

together, and as for being both at once he could never be, yet or ever."

"I hate to think of leaving before the mystery of Grand Pierre is solved."

"Me too, but then if he is still missing when we come down next year we will undoubtedly solve it then."

"Perhaps," said Alice. "And perhaps not. We have had successes in the past but that does not mean that we will always have them. Our luck up to this time has been extraordinary, but that does not mean it always will be."

"Oh yes it does," said Gertrude firmly. "We have trod on a lucky herb in our lives."

At that moment Johnny-jump-up appeared in the kitchen doorway.

"Ah Johnny," said Alice, "good morning and what do you want for breakfast?"

"Anything your sweet heart conceives," he said. "You are the *petit déjeuner* expert par excellence. I must have put on three kilos while I have been here."

"We were just talking about your poor Claude," said Gertrude. "And I said I thought P'tit Pierre was a victim but Alice thought he might be a manipulator."

"Hardly," said Johnny. "I do not think he's developed that far."

"It's raining a little," said Gertrude, "and that means no sunbathing today and no walks on our turns, either uphill or down, it's too muddly."

"Muddy," said Alice.

"I like muddly," said Gertrude. "It sounds more like what it really is."

"Whatever it is," said Johnny, "it's still beautiful. The leaves have turned and the valley is full of red and gold and brown and ocher."

"It is the season of mists and mellow fruitfulness," said Alice, quoting Keats.

"And all fruit filled with ripeness to the core," Gertrude continued.

"While autumn, drowsed with the fume of poppies," Alice went on, "sits on the furrow sound asleep."

"Well," said Johnny, dusting his hands, "that pretty well takes care of Keats and the fall of the year."

"Except for the gnats mourning along the river and the hedge-crickets singing," said Alice.

"Keats was the best," said Gertrude. "If that silly Leigh Hunt had just left him alone."

"To leave poesy for the moment," said Alice, "whilst I ready your breakfast, will you take Chen up to his room and apply some calamine lotion to his arm. He has picked up a bit of poison ivy somewhere."

"Of course," said Johnny, and beckoned to Chen. "I will fix your arm," he said in French to the Annamite lad.

Chen put down the pot, smiled and made two half-bows to Gertrude and Alice, and they went upstairs to the slanted attic above Johnny's room, where Chen slept. It was a bare room with a bed, a few books, and a small window set in the steeper slope of the mansard roof. The view looked out over the great plane tree near the front gate.

"Please remove your chemise," Johnny said in French.

Chen was a small handsome young man with a slender body. His straight black hair gleamed with a sort of blue shine in the dull light. Suddenly he was attractive to Johnny, who aside from Claude, had had no romantic encounters during the ten days of his visit — save, of course, with old Mrs. Palm and her five daughters. In the soft light, the golden tone of Chen's young torso seemed more than desirable. And then, with a winsome smile, Johnny reached to loosen Chen's belt buckle. The young man's body on the dark coverlet looked like that of a tawny Ganymede, slim and charming.

When Johnny had finished his small offering to Eros, he applied the lotion and bandaged the arm, and together they went hand in hand down the attic stairs, and then down the stone ones to the kitchen.

"Did you fix him up?" asked Alice.

"I did indeed," said Johnny, running his tongue halfway across his upper lip. "But when I first looked at his skin I thought he might have yellow jaundice. And then I remembered he was Annamite."

Alice chuckled. "Amusing," she said.

But Johnny was lost in wonder, for he had never realized that Oriental pubic hair could be straight instead of curled.

❧ XIV ❧

Interview with a Popinjay

EVERYWHERE IN ALICE'S WORKROOM was a clutter of books, piled in corners, on bookshelves and tables and the floor. In the middle of the largest table stood the massive Smith-Premier typewriter which Gertrude had acquired many years before, after she had disposed of her ancient Blickensdörfer on which the *s* and *e* keys stuck against the letter that followed them. There Alice typed everything, being one of the few persons who could accurately decipher Gertrude's hentrack handwriting.

The telephone beside the typewriter jangled three times before Alice would get to it. Gertrude never answered the telephone for she hated to speak French over it, feeling that she needed French gestures to complete and supplement French talk.

"Mademoiselle Toklas écoute," said Alice, picking up the receiver.

"Je m'appelle Monsieur Duvalle, Hercule Duvalle," said the voice. "I am the policier who is currently assisting Monsieur Gallos in the matter of the disappearance of Monsieur Desjardins. I am wondering if you and Mademoiselle Stein would be free enough and willing to permit me to have a brief interview with you at two this afternoon."

Alice never accepted the first-mentioned hour for anything or anyone. "Would it be convenient for you to come at three instead of two?" she asked.

"D'accord," said Monsieur Duvalle. He sounded pleasant enough over the phone — a deep voice in which one could sense a residual authority.

Alice carried the news to Gertrude that the policier was coming.

"What on earth for," Gertrude asked.

"I suppose he wants to see from what vantage point we saw Grand Pierre and Debat on that Monday morning," Alice said.

"It is exciting, that's what it is," said Gertrude. "It is like visiting the scene of the crime. And since his first name is Hercule I am already in favor of him because of Agatha, and since her Hercule always solved everything, this one is bound to too."

"Do not judge the book by its cover, nor the dick by his monicker," said Alice.

"Your vocabulary certainly has suffered from all those years in San Francisco," said Gertrude.

"Look who's talking," Alice said. "Pots and kettles."

"Nevertheless," said Gertrude.

Monsieur Duvalle arrived promptly as the tiny clock on the salon mantel chimed the third note of three. Alice met him at the gate. There was handshaking and bowing, and Alice led the way around the corner of the house to the French windows of the living room.

He was a very small dapper man dressed in a shiny black suit and wearing a papillon, a bow-tie. He had a thin pointed face and an enormous mustache, in which threads of grey mingled with the black. His ears were quite large.

Gertrude was sitting in her wicker rocker, and half-rose to shake his hand.

"You are very kind to grant me this interview," said Duvalle.

"It is our pleasure," said Gertrude.

"I have read the autobiography of Mademoiselle Toklas," said Duvalle, and Gertrude began to beam.

"I found it absorbing but rather frivolous," said Duvalle, and Gertrude's beaming stopped.

"Ah yes," she said and was silent.

"I am here to see, if you will permit," Monsieur Duvalle went on, unaware that with seven words he had cast himself into the outer darkness, "the place from which you witnessed Monsieur Desjardins on a Monday morning some weeks ago."

Alice was also looking thunderous, but she remembered her training. "We shall be pleased to show you," she said a bit stiffly, and the three of them went into the garden.

"It was from this wall," said Alice. "If you look down to your left you will see the fields of Debat."

"Ah yes," said Duvalle. "Might one also be privileged to see the lunette d'approche through which you surveyed the field and the figures?"

"But of a certainty," said Alice, retreating to the house and emerging with the spyglass.

Hercule looked at it admiringly and pulled it to its full length. "It is a work of art," he said.

How would you know, thought Gertrude.

"It is quite old but still serviceable," said Alice.

Gertrude uttered not a word.

"You use it to spy upon your neighbors?" asked Hercule.

"Hardly," said Alice. "I am a bird-watcher."

"Ah yes," said Duvalle with a disbelieving inflection.

"And Mademoiselle Stein uses it to check on the snow-level on Mont Blanc," said Alice, "to see if we can expect rain or a great deal of water in Switzerland."

Hercule focused the spyglass on the fields. "It jiggles," he said.

"You must be nervous," said Alice. "Perhaps there was an overabundance of wine last night?"

"I do not drink," said Hercule, a bit shortly.

"Does our presence then disturb you?" queried Alice.

"Not in the least," said Duvalle. "I have met many men and women before."

Alice looked at Gertrude, who was stony.

"Could it be that your age caused a trembling?" Duvalle went on. "Can you be sure that it was indeed Desjardins who approached Debat that day?"

Alice reached for the spyglass, and pulled it so sharply from his eye that it dug into his cheekbone.

"Oh, I am sorry," she said apologetically. "But realizing the tremors, I rested it on the wall. Like this," she said, and knelt on the gravel, putting the glass against the edge. Rising, she handed it back to him. "If you try it that way, your vision might be more clear and steady."

Gertrude stood with folded arms, saying nothing.

Duvalle knelt and tried the spyglass in that position. "Ah," he said. "Everything is now quite obvious." He rose and dusted his knee. "Have you lived here long?" he asked.

"Some years," said Alice. Gertrude had turned meanwhile and was inspecting a rose bush.

"Alice," she said sharply in English. "There are bugs on this plant."

"I'll tell Petit Pierre," said Alice.

"Is either of you married?" asked Duvalle. "Or have you been?"

"No," said Alice. "We have found most candidates somewhat stupid." Like your question, she added under her breath.

Duvalle said nothing. Then after a pause he spoke. "You would be able to recognize Desjardins at such a distance?"

"We have lived next to him in Bilignin long enough not to make a mistake," Alice said. "Is there anything else you wish to ask?"

"At the moment, no," said Duvalle. "You have been most helpful. I will go now to interview his son."

"It would be wise to take paper and pencil," said Alice, "for you know he is a deaf-mute."

"But of course," said Duvalle. Alice walked him to the gate. Gertrude had disappeared into the house without saying farewell.

"What a nest of vipers," thought Duvalle as he went toward the Desjardins dwelling.

When Alice returned to the livingroom, Gertrude was all thundercloud and lightning. And Alice herself was furious. They turned and stood facing each other for a long moment.

Finally Gertrude spoke.

"A real son of a bitch," she said. "I shall never again read another word of Agatha's."

"What a funny little man he was," said Alice. "A popinjay."

They both laughed.

"Like the Marquess of Queensbury, I betcha," said Gertrude. "I will never again think harshly of Lord Alfred."

❧ XV ❧

Tally-Ho!

JOHNNY WAS IN THE BATHROOM the next morning, brushing his teeth, when he heard a commotion next door in the bedroom of Gertrude and Alice. There was first the sound of something being overturned, and then Gertrude's great contralto voice came booming through the bedroom door and the wall that adjoined the bathroom, begging and pleading, with even a note of panic in it riding high over the tumult.

"Oh don't Pussy, don't please don't. I'll promise to do anything, Pussy, anything at all, but please, please, don't do it. Please, Pussy. Please, don't. I'll be good, I promise. Oh, Pussy, please don't. Please stop."

Paralyzed, his toothbrush arrested against his front incisors, Johnny heard and was shocked. Visions of Sapphic horrors rushed through his head. *What* in the world was going on? He envisioned them naked and Gertrude being tortured in some strange and violent way.

Just at that moment the bedroom door burst open and Gertrude — fully clothed — rushed from the room, a look of utter panic on her face. A scant three feet behind her came Alice, holding a large brilliant peacock feather. She reached forth with it and tickled the nape of Gertrude's neck, and then her ear. Gertrude yelled with a kind of sobbing laughter, and Alice was grinning from here to there.

"Ha!" exclaimed Alice. "No one is going to tell me how to make cornmeal mush ever again, not ever! I don't care how your Aunt Pauline used to make it, I will go on making it with water, not milk!"

They stopped short on seeing Johnny, and both burst into wild laughter.

"I — I can't stand being tickled," gasped Gertrude, panting. "And she knows it and always does it when she wants to win an argument."

Alice was giggling. "And I always w-win w-when I do," she said, and threw her arms around Gertrude's ample figure, hugging her.

"For heaven's sake," said Johnny, "I thought something horrible was going on."

Gertrude disengaged herself, still chortling. "And so did Hemingway once when he stopped in at the rue Fleurus all unexpected and heard the same thing going on upstairs, and he went away without knowing what was going on and while that was not the beginning of the end it was really the ending of the end, and we saw him again after that but it was never the same, and then the hair grew on his chest and he started to examine it and paw around through it and write about it, and that was really and truly the end of Hemingway."

Gradually they all calmed down except for some heavy breathing, and Gertrude's tanned face resumed its usual color.

"Well," said Alice, still a bit short of breath. "And what would you like for breakfast, Johnny?"

"Cornmeal mush," said Johnny, and off they went once more into gales of giggling.

So Alice set about making it in the kitchen, and when it was done — all on the great heavy tray, gleaming with silver pots and silver cutlery and white napery and golden steaming mush and real maple syrup and yellow country butter in a silver pot, with a delicious spotted banana and a slice of Algerian melon and some of the wonderful French roast coffee — she brought it proudly to Johnny in the grey living room amongst the trompe l'oeil hunting horns and fruits painted on the walls.

"There — eat," she said, putting the tray down on the wicker table. "And enjoy."

When Johnny was finished, he rolled the last morsel of the sweet fragrant melon over his talented tongue and sighed. The sun was out this day, and there were great low masses of white clouds against the horizon. What to do on such a day?

Gertrude trod heavily into the room. The glass droplets around a little lampshade tinkled faintly from her stride.

"All finished," she asked, and saw that he was. "Then," she said, "what do you say to visiting the possibly real scene of the really possible crime."

"D'accord," he said, nodding.

"We will take the two dogs and go down to the forested end of Debat's field and see if there is anything to be found, that is, provided Debat isn't around."

In the kitchen Alice heard her and came hastily into the salon. "Indeed you will not," she said. "I have just bathed and combed Basket, and to take him down amongst the briars and brambles will mean I'll have to do it all over again. He will come back and that long white poodle hair will be full of burrs and sticky things. He would have to be shaved after such an excursion."

"Then we'll just take Pepe," said Gertrude. "Nothing sticks to him."

"All right," said Alice, retreating through the dining-room.

"Are you ready, Johnny," Gertrude asked.

"Quite."

And so they were off, Gertrude seizing one of her Korean straw hats from the rack as she left, and a dog-leash with which she liked to switch off the heads of weeds and thistles as she went.

It was a treacherous climb down the hillside, away from their usual path. The weeds and undergrowth pulled at their clothes, and Johnny had to duck frequently because Gertrude let fly the low-hanging branches of trees in their passing.

They talked of many things on the way down.

"Now you take Coleridge," she said. "In a kind of way he and Poe are the same, very much the same."

"How's that?" asked Johnny, always the straight man (although he hated the word), or perhaps the Boswell.

"Their narrative poetry is so simply pure that the narrative and the poetry are really one. It is disembodied poetry, the pure stuff, the real thing."

"I like the Xanadu fragment," said Johnny. "If there is anything that would ever turn me completely against religion it is the vicar from Porlock who interrupted the composition of it. The last lines are really great, the ones that begin 'Beware, beware! his flashing eyes, his floating hair . . .' "

"Yes, they're wonderful," said Gertrude. And then she spoke of Wordsworth, poor Wordsworth, and how disappointed she had been when recently re-reading the immortality ode, and so gradually they reached the level ground beside Debat's field, and walked the length of its grasses toward the forest that edged the far end of his field. There was no one to be seen anywhere.

"Let us walk through the woods there and have a look," said Gertrude. Her voice had dropped in decibels, into an almost conspiratorial level.

"All right," said Johnny in the same low key.

There was hardly a path. Pepe bounded along beside them, sometimes in front, sometimes behind to investigate a cow-disc or a brown slug. Sometimes he yapped when he saw a squirrel or a field mouse.

Since there was no path, Gertrude picked the thinnest undergrowth she could see, plunging ahead with Johnny following close behind.

"Good heavens," she said, "it's as thick as can be."

But they went on. Occasionally there was a small clearing, deep with fallen leaves, all browning and dying, breathing their last on the heavy loam, which was still a little damp from the light rainfall of a few days past.

"If anyone wanted to hide anything this would be the place to do it, wooden it now," Gertrude grumbled after they had penetrated about a hundred meters into the forest.

"Yes," said Johnny. He was beginning to wish the expedition might be over, for his hands were dirty and scratched, and his shoes a mess. His back ached, and his leg muscles were unaccountably sore from the steep trip down the hillside.

Suddenly with a series of penetrating shrill yappings Pepe dashed in front of them to a spot a few centimeters removed from a bush on which grew a profusion of red berries. Both Gertrude and Johnny were startled.

"Come away from there, Pepe," Gertrude ordered, and started toward him. Johnny laid a hand on her arm.

"No, wait a moment," he said.

"I can't, he's probably found a dead animal and he may eat it and get some sort of poison," said Gertrude, pulling away.

"Please wait," said Johnny, amazed at his boldness in even daring to restrain her. "There's nothing there — see, except dead leaves that he's scraping away."

"You're right," said Gertrude. "What on earth can he be after."

"You said he likes fromage," said Johnny jokingly. "Perhaps he's found an old Stilton someone discarded."

Pepe continued to paw the ground. He had scattered the leaves and was furiously at work digging with his tiny paws at the soft earth. Deeper and deeper he went, until his small tail and half his hindquarters were all that could be seen above ground.

Gertrude and Johnny stood close over him, fascinated.

"Buried treasure, do you suppose?" Johnny asked.

"Buried something," said Gertrude.

And then Pepe got hold of what looked like a fabric rope of some sort, and Johnny fell to his knees on the ground to help Pepe at his arduous task. Pepe growled, but permitted him to come to his aid.

Johnny grasped the fabric and pulled on it. Dirt fell off in great and small clods. Slowly he lifted it upward.

It was the handle of a large-netted filet, the sort of reusable shopping container of heavy string that Frenchwomen carry instead of brown paper bags. And it was filled with merchandise of various sorts, small wrapped parcels.

"My God," said Gertrude softly.

"Indeed," said Johnny. "It's Grand Pierre's purchases from Belley."

❧ XVI ❧

An Inventory of Something Dirty

"WHAT IN THE WORLD shall we do with it?" Johnny asked.

The excitement had caused Gertrude's palms to sweat. She wiped them on her skirt. "We should by rights not touch anything at all, we should call the police at once, maybe one of us should go for the cops, at least that's what they always say."

Johhny was a little pale beneath his tan. "But if one of us goes and Debat should happen to come, he will know — if he did it — that he's in grave danger, and he might kill the guardian."

"You are right," said Gertrude. "I would hate to be alone with him and I would be no match for him and neither would you as far as that goes, he's a big man."

Johnny was holding the filet, still dislodging clods and clumps from itself as it swung slowly around in his hand. Pepe was yapping shrilly and leaping upward, trying to catch it with his teeth.

"Quiet Pepe," Gertrude shouted and then reached down

to pick him up. He struggled fiercely to escape and get at the filet once again.

"Whatever do you suppose excites him so?" asked Johnny.

Gertrude thought a moment, then brightened. "It's the cheese of course, he's mad about cheese, any kind, and that was one of the things Grand Pierre bought that day, it must still be in there, and that's why he started digging for it and really why we found it."

"Two of the things," said Johnny. "He bought some camembert and also some cheap cheese for the spaghetti noodles, remember."

"So he did," said Gertrude. "Well, there's only one thing to do. Two things. We'll take the filet back to the house and see what's in it and then call the cops."

"And the second thing?"

"I'll hold Pepe and you put the filet on the ground and kick the earth back in the hole and spread some leaves over it again and then we'll go."

Johnny kicked at the earth and got most of it back. Then he gathered some leaves and spread them casually over the spot. It looked quite undisturbed.

"By rights," he said, "we should leave a trail of bread-crumbs or something so that we can find the spot again if we come here with the cops."

"I just don't happen to have any breadcrumbs handy," said Gertrude. "We will take a careful glance around and then see where we come out of the woods so that we can get back in without too much trouble. Have you got any paper maybe, we might tear it up and drop little pieces here and there."

"Not a scrap," said Johnny, "but I can always put my Boy Scout training to good use."

"How will that help," asked Gertrude. She swatted the complaining Pepe gently on his rump. "Do stop, Pepe, there's a good boy."

"I can break off a branch here and there and leave it sort of dangling. That way it wouldn't be noticed as much as if it were broken off entirely. And I can pile three stones together on the way out in several places."

"Good," said Gertrude. "And I will carry Pepe and you can carry the filet."

"Then let's go," said Johnny.

Getting out seemed to take forever. At intervals of about ten feet Johnny would break a twig or a branch and leave it hanging from a bush, and then for the next interval he would arrange three stones in a small triangle. They moved very quietly, and Gertrude finally in desperation clamped one hand around Pepe's muzzle to keep him from barking so much. He protested violently but subsided after a few moments, and Gertrude took her hand away.

Slowly then, with many fearful glances around, they came to the edge of the forest and into the bright sunlight once again. There was no one to be seen in Debat's field, nor indeed anywhere. They took the path back up the hill to the château.

"Glory," said Gertrude, puffing. "This damned dog must weigh twenty kilos by now, it seems like."

"Tell you what," said Johnny. "Let me carry him for a while and you take the filet."

So it was done. The air was sweet and a vagrant breeze swept gently over the fields as they trudged slowly upward. And finally they reached the path beside the château. Just as they did, Gertrude looked alarmed, and felt in her capacious pockets.

"Good fathers," she said. "Somewhere down there I

dropped the leash or left it where we found the filet."

"Oh my," said Johnny, dismayed. "Shall I go back for it?"

"No, no," said Gertrude. "We have been lucky so far, let us not stretch our good fortune. Perhaps no one will find it until we come with the police."

"You must be sure to tell them you left it down there," said Johnny, "or they might think you were the guilty party."

"Don't worry, I will," said Gertrude.

They went around the side of the house to the garden. Johnny put Pepe down on the ground, and he at once resumed his shrill barking. Alice heard him and came to the door and looked out.

"Where in the world have you two been so long?" she said.

"Pussy, oh Pussy," Gertrude said. "Come here, come here at once and look what we found."

Alice drew near and looked at the misshapen thing. "It's a filet full of stuff," she said.

"It is *the* filet, you ninny," said Gertrude. "The one that Grand Pierre was carrying that morning."

Alice gasped, took a second deep breath, and staggered toward the garden wall to sit down. "Oh good heavens," she said. "This is the tangible that the policier said must be found. It's not a dead body, but it's the next thing to it."

Then Gertrude paled, too. "Oh," she said. "That means you are now involved. Deep."

"You mean we both are," said Alice.

Johnny realized that something had to be done to stop the panic which he felt settling on them. He knelt by the filet. "Well, we should at least see what's here," he said, "even though the police might not want us to touch anything." He looked up. "Do you have the lists we took to Belley?"

"I have mine," said Alice.

"I've lost mine," said Gertrude, "but I can remember."

"I think I can too," said Johnny. "Let's see — " and he very carefully extracted a longish bundle from the filet, leaving the dirt on it, and peered down the open end of the paper wrapping. "Here are the noodles," he said. "A little limp, but still there."

"That's one of my items," said Alice. Her fingers were fluttering, and she now and then placed the tips of them together, a thing she always did when nervously upset.

"And here," said Johnny, extracting two small paper-wrapped packages and squeezing them gently, "are what Pepe was after — one of them camembert — " he sniffed at it and quickly took it from his nose — "ooh, what a stink! And the other, not so bad." He smelled at it too.

"There should be some butter," said Alice. Johnny poked at the other packages.

"Not here," he said.

"I suppose Debat took that to eat," said Gertrude.

"Then why not the cheese as well?" asked Alice.

"Maybe he didn't like cheese," said Johnny, poking still more. "And the bread is gone also."

"Bread and butter," said Gertrude.

"And here are some nails," said Johnny. "And a paint brush. And some bicycle wheel spokes. And that seems to be all."

"Then what's missing," Gertrude asked.

"Well," said Johnny, sitting back on his heels, "From my list there was the snuff and the Gitane cigarettes, and the small paring knife."

"He could have put the snuff and the cigarettes in his pocket," said Alice, "and maybe he kept the paring knife too."

"That's all then, isn't it," asked Gertrude.

"I think so," Johnny and Alice said in unison, and Johnny giggled a little nervously.

"Now we'd better call Capitaine Gallos in Belley," Gertrude said. "You talk to him, Pussy."

"Oh, all right," said Alice, somewhat petulant. "But I won't talk to that horrible Duvalle again, you can bet on that."

"When are you two planning to go back to Paris?" Johnny asked, getting up from the ground.

Gertrude and Alice looked at each other.

"We weren't planning to go until the middle of October," Gertrude said. "That's about three weeks off."

"If I were you — " Johnny began.

"Yes, yes," said Alice. "If we can get ready we may go sooner than that."

"This is closer than we've ever come to being really involved," said Gertrude. "And I think Alice may be right, we may leave sooner. I wouldn't mind if we left tomorrow morning, not a bit."

"I'll call Belley," said Alice. "And Johnny, please bring the filet in. We'll put it high on the cupboard so Pepe can't get at it."

Johnny picked it up and took it into the kitchen. Alice pulled out a chair and some newspapers, and handed them to him. He climbed up on it to reach the top of the cupboard. "Put the papers underneath," she advised. "It's so dirty."

Gertrude stood in the doorway watching. "Why don't

you wait until after lunch to call," she said. "I'm hungry and it's almost noon, and if I don't eat regular, I don't stay regular."

Alice sighed. "I'd like to put it off as long as possible," she said.

"Then we'll eat slow," said Gertrude, "and fletcherize."

"What's that, for goodness' sake?" asked Johnny.

"You're too young to know," said Alice. "He was a quack who said you had to chew every mouthful twenty-eight times."

"Well," he said, "the gendarmerie closes at four-thirty, and at that rate we may not be through by then."

"It would suit me fine," said Alice.

❧ XVII ❧

Lunch and an Insult

THE LUNCH WAS LOVELY.

They started with cold Chinese eggs, cooked hard in sherry, then put into a casserole and further cooked with soy sauce until dark brown. Alice had cut some of the sliced and garnished bread of the Bugey into small triangles to serve with them, along with a dab of parsleyed mayonnaise.

"Yummy," said Gertrude as she finished her second egg.

"You're not fletcherizing," said Alice.

"How can I," said Gertrude. "They're too good."

Then there was sole à la Ritz — prepared quite simply, poached in hot water. Alice passed around a small dish of sauce.

"What's in this," Gertrude asked.

"Whipped cream with horseradish," said Alice.

"I'll certainly need a digestive after all this," said Gertrude.

"I'll let you have some benedictine," said Alice. "A thimbleful. And Johnny too."

"Gracious," Johnny murmured.

"I'd say stingy," said Gertrude.

They savored the delicate flavors of the fish and sauce in silence, but even Alice smacked her lips.

Finally they had all rested their forks and fish knives. Alice held up her fish knife.

"Francis gave us these," she said.

"He swiped them from the family baronial estate," said Gertrude. "He's not very moral."

"He is really very wicked," said Alice. "Wickeder than you, Johnny, and lots more evil."

"Johnny's a good boy," said Gertrude. "He's bashful and smart and maybe devious and he blushes a lot, but he's good."

"Aw," said Johnny.

"Do we have vegetables or a salad or both," Gertrude asked.

"Both in one," said Alice.

Chen took away their plates in silence and then brought the salad. It was tiny buds of fresh cauliflower mixed with bits of sliced cucumber and chickpeas.

"Salade Livonière," said Alice. "The dressing is French mustard and brandy and Madeira, oil and vinegar, and salt and pepper." To Johnny she passed a tiny jeweled cloisonné swan of red, blue, and green with an open back, in which rested salt crystals. "You'll need some more salt, Johnny," she said. "Gertrude has to watch hers."

"It's delicious as is," said Johnny, but he took a pinch of salt anyway.

Then there came the tiny glasses of benedictine. Johnny tasted the fiery drops, rolling them on his tongue while the fumes mounted upward through his head, velvety and rumbling, yet with a golden tenderness like a violoncello in a minor key.

"And now," said Gertrude, "it's after two o'clock, why not call Monsieur Gallos and not tell him anything, just that we have found some new information that may be important, and no, we don't want to tell him over the phone, it's a party line, and could he come tomorrow at ten, and then if you can do it, tell him not to bring that Hercule what's-his-name with him, but Claude his secretary . . . "

" . . . if Claude can walk by now," said Johnny.

"Yes, and then Johnny and I will stand at the door and give you all the support and courage that you need."

Alice sighed, and they all went to workroom. She checked the number for the gendarmerie in Belley, and picked up the receiver.

"Allo," she said to the operator. "Dix-neuf, soixante-neuf, zero," she said.

And then: "Allo . . . puis-je parler avec Monsieur Gallos?" She covered the mouthpiece. "It sounded like young Claude, but painfully so . . . No . . . thank you . . . it is a private matter. I would prefer to speak directly with Monsieur Gallos."

"Monsieur Gallos? . . . This is Mademoiselle Alice Toklas here, with Mademoiselle Stein, who came to see you the other day . . . Yes, thank you, quite well . . ."

She listened for a moment, then said: "You are a very amiable . . . Mademoiselle Stein and I have learned of some new things which we feel should be brought to your attention . . . yes, concerning the disappearance of Monsieur Desjardins . . . No, it is too long a history and we would prefer not to speak of it over the appareil, since there are others on the line . . . yes, I am sure you will understand. I am wondering if you would be so kind as to call on us in Bilignin tomorrow morning at ten hours, if that is convenient with you ... and Monsieur, would you be so kind as to wear walking shoes, and perhaps you would bring your secretary ... Oh, he has had an accident? I am sorry to hear that ... is he well by now? And he will be able to come with you? Good ... That is very kind of you, Monsieur Gallos ... "

And here Gertrude and Johnny saw Alice draw up her shoulders, and actually seem to become larger and firmer, as she said: "No, we would prefer that you not bring Monsieur Duvalle, because ... both Mademoiselle Stein and myself have found him — "

And then she said what was the second greatest phrase of insult to be heard in all of France, one which called upon the totality of French culture, tradition, politeness, and social grace, and said the horrifying words:

"Because, Monsieur Gallos, both Mademoiselle Stein and myself have found him to be *très peu gentil.*"

Gertrude gasped. "The prime insult in France!" She permitted herself an exclamation point.

"Very little ... genteel?" said Johnny, puzzled.

" 'Gentil' means much more than that,' said Gertrude. "She has cast him into the outer darkness. To say that of a person is the greatest condemnation, it means no breeding, no manners, no savoir faire, no nothing. Oh, oh."

Alice hung up the receiver and looked around. Her face was flushed but triumphant, and she was smiling.

"Monsieur Gallos must have dropped the handset," she said. "There was a loud clatter, then silence, and when he spoke again it was in great confusion."

"I think Duvalle will not dare show his face around here ever," said Gertrude happily.

"At least not while we're in residence," said Alice.

"How will Monsieur Gallos stop him from coming along tomorrow," asked Gertrude.

"He will undoubtedly send him on some fool's errand," said Alice. "Well, Lovey, we've done it again."

"And incidentally given me," said Johnny, "one of the great and useful phrases of all time."

"Do not tell it to any American tourists," cautioned Alice. "It is a French insult, of the French, by the French, and for the French, to be used on the French. If Americans start to use it, it will lose all of its zing. By the way, Johnny, do you have any sleeping pills? Will you be able to sleep tonight, with all this excitement?"

"Don't worry about me," said Johnny, thinking of the nearly untouched emergency bottle of Courvoisier in his suitcase upstairs. A few good belts would take care of any sleeplessness. "Do you need some pills yourselves?" he asked.

Gertrude looked at Alice lovingly. "I think we won't," she said, and put her arm around Alice's shoulders.

❦ XVIII ❦

A Little Dog Shall Lead Them

PROMPTLY AT TEN THE NEXT MORNING Monsieur Gallos arrived, dressed in his official dark blue uniform but wearing some heavy brown shoes, which certainly did not go well with the uniform and the round billed cap of office. His mustache was abristle and eyes penetrating. With him came Claude limping, pad and pencil in one hand, and in the other a cane. Poor Claude's face was at the moment a disaster — one eye had turned a violent yellow and blue in its surroundings, and the color had seeped across the bridge of his nose to the other eye. His lip was still a little fat.

"Mesdemoiselles," said Monsieur, "I am at your service." He bowed slightly.

"We are enchanted to see you," said Gertrude, shaking his hand. "And Monsieur McAndrews from America, our good friend."

"Enchanté," said Gallos to him, bowing and shaking hands again.

"We have unearthed," said Alice, "an object which may be of significance to you."

"And what is that?" asked Gallos.

Alice retreated to the kitchen and appeared shortly bearing the filet, clods and all, on a piece of newspaper which she carefully deposited on the dining room table.

"Regardez donc," she said.

"Mais qu'est-ce-c'est que cela?" inquired Monsieur Gallos.

"Ah," said Gertrude.

"It is the filet containing the verified purchases, or most of them, made by Pierre Desjardins, Grand Pierre, in Belley on the Monday morning in question."

"Where did you find it?" asked Gallos.

"Mademoiselle Stein and Monsieur McAndrews discovered it on a morning walk," said Alice. "It was buried deep in the forest that adjoins the wintergrain field of Monsieur Debat, under a bush with red berries."

"Why did you not leave it until I could have arrived to see it?"

Gertrude spoke up. "We had no way of knowing if whoever had buried it might not return whilst one of us went to inform you," she said. "We debated the topic sérieusement, and decided to bring it here for your investigation. Monsieur McAndrews very carefully put the soil back into the cavity, the hole, and covered it with leaves again, and we brought it to the house in great concern and fear, at our risks and perils. And on the return, I discovered that I had left the dog-leash there, possibly in the area of discovery."

"Ah yes," said Monsieur Gallos, twirling his mustache points. "Under the circumstances I believe that you acted correctly with concern for your own safety, although the law in most cases is very clear: the evidence must not be touched save by authorized persons."

"So it is, and that we knew," said Alice. "But you were

not there and telephonic communication between the forest and Belley was unfortunately impossible."

Monsieur Gallos smiled. "Understood," he said. "There is no censure of your actions." He poked around in the filet. "You have then inventoried the contents?"

"That we have," said Gertrude. "All seems to be there except the bread and butter, a small paring knife from the Exquisite Hardware, the Gitane cigarettes and the snuff, the tabac prisé — which he had possibly placed in his pocket. Logically, that would be expected."

"Bien," said Monsieur Gallos. "Quite so, truly."

He turned to them. "Would it then be possible for us to see the spot where you found the filet, down there in the forest?"

"But of course," said Alice.

"It is a trip downhill and back," said Johnny, speaking for the first time. "Can it be that your secretary is able to walk that far?"

Monsieur Gallos turned to Claude. "You will be able?"

Claude smiled rather wanly. "I believe that yes," he asked. "If I cannot, I will pause and await your return."

"Shall we then begin our expedition?"

There was a small flurry of preparation. Gertrude seized the blackthorne shillelagh, long enough to be used as a walking stick, a gift from James Joyce, after the one occasion when they had met at Sylvia Beach's bookstore.

It was a strange procession, and anyone looking up from the valley below would have been astonished to see them silhouetted against the sky, walking in single file down the hill. First came a tiny dog almost obscured by the grasses, led on a leash by a stocky female figure; then a very short bent lady in black, followed by a military outline [or that of a *flic* with a pompier's billed cap], and after him a young male figure limping with a cane. The rear was brought up by a tall lean young man, stumbling a bit over the uneven terrain. The procession moved slowly and yet with purpose.

Gertrude was talking over her shoulder to Gallos. "We left a Boy Scout trail, that is Johnny did, so that we could find the place again without much trouble, and the spot is well concealed with leaves and dirt."

"That is to be commended," said Gallos. "You have been very careful. But I am greatly concerned about one thing."

"And what is that?"

"If Monsieur Debat should be arrested," said Gallos. "It means that Mademoiselle Toklas who saw him with the spyglass will then be an important witness."

"If Debat is in custody, then I am relatively safe," said Alice.

"But it means that without your testimony, there is no case or very little of one. And without a body, the case is still very feeble."

"That, I understand," said Alice. "And there is still another thing."

"And what is that?" asked Gallos.

"Mademoiselle Stein and I are accustomed to leave Bilignin quite soon for our winter in Paris, in our home. What will happen then?"

There was a lengthened silence, broken only by the sound of their steps crunching against the terrain and the small rocks. Then Gallos spoke.

"If a body should be found, and if there should be a trial, it will be imperative for Mademoiselle Toklas to be here for it. There will be a subpoena issued, directing her to return under penalty. But that might well be delayed until the mesdemoiselles come back next spring. Justice turns slowly, leisurely, in la belle France."

From her frontal position Gertrude spoke. "Is there not such a thing as a deposition, whereby Mademoiselle Toklas can swear to what she saw, and would it not for the moment take care of her wintertime return."

"It might," said Gallos. "It would depend on the strength of the evidence and the disposition and even the whim of the magistrate, or perhaps what he had for lunch. But a deposition will quite possibly be necessary before your departure."

"I am certain," said Alice, "that a courtroom and the giving of testimony would make me extremely nervous."

"As it does all," said Gallos. "But Mademoiselle need not fear. In such a preliminary hearing, which is what the first one would be, there is no cross-examination and the magistrate is quite gentle. Moreover, I would caution him ahead of time."

"Que vous êtes tout à fait aimable," murmured Alice.

By then they had reached the edge of the forest. They had seen no one in Debat's field.

"We entered here between these two large bushes," Gertrude announced, and Pepe barked twice. "Johnny," she said. "You must come now and lead the way and look for your Boy Scout signs."

Johnny left his position at the rear of the queue and came forward. He looked to the right and left. "It is this way," he said, noticing a dangling twig on a bush to the right.

Before they went into the woods Gallos looked at the neatly plowed furrows of Debat's field. "What is planted in there?" he asked. "What does he cultivate?"

"Wintergrain of some sort," said Alice. "Planted now, it lies dormant until spring and then arises. It may be winter-wheat, or perhaps barley."

"Ah yes," said Gallos and turned toward the forest.

Johnny led the way, without any trouble finding the signs he had left every ten feet.

"What a Boy Scout I am," he said sotto voce. Gertrude heard him.

"You are many things," said Gertrude, chuckling a little. "But a Boy Scout you are not, it might be better to call you a Davy Crockett or a Natty Bumppo."

"Those are strange words," said Gallos.

"They were trackers and adventurers in tales from the American West," Alice explained.

Suddenly Gertrude whooped, startling them all. "There's my dog leash," she said, and sure enough, there it lay like a thin coiled black snake on the ground.

"And there," said Johnny, "is the bush with the red berries. And here, Monsieur Gallos," he said, brushing aside some leaves with his foot, "is the spot."

"One can see that the ground has been disturbed," said Alice.

"Ah yes," said Gallos. "How deeply was it buried?"

Gertrude picked up Pepe and turned him upside down, head toward the ground. He protested. "Down to here," she said, pointing to the middle of his back flank. "He dug until only his derrière and tail were to be seen."

"This is excellent," said Gallos. "I shall now return to my headquarters and seek out the Judge Sulpice to ask for a mandat for the arrest on suspicion of Monsieur Debat."

"And I," said Alice, "will go home and bar the gate and lock the doors and windows."

"Never fear," said Johnny. "I am there to protect you."

"Phoo," said Gertrude, and in English added. "They'll give us a matron."

"Maybe a gendarme," said Johnny. "A *flic* lithe and handsome, with curly black hair."

"Then he'd be the one who'd never get out alive," said Gertrude amused.

They all started back up the hill again.

❧ XIX ❧

Of Littles and Lots

ALICE WAS IN HER WORKROOM busily putting things into a large cardboard box. Somewhat hastily and with no concern for order or sequence she was throwing pencils into it, some pens, erasers, some white stationery and some blue — but then she carefully took out the blue, because in the tiniest of white letters it had "Bilignin, France" printed at the top.

"Basta!" she said, picking up still more rubber bands, carbon paper, paper clips and all the detritus one might expect to find on a secretary's desk.

"Did I hear you say 'bastard'?" queried Johnny from the doorway, where he stood fiddling with a cigarette.

"No, you did not," said Alice, somewhat grumpily. Packing to leave for Paris was a yearly chore she thoroughly despised. "I said 'basta' which is a perfectly respectable Italian and Spanish word meaning 'Enough' or 'No more.' And that's exactly the way I feel about it."

"Can I be of some help?" asked Johnny.

"Yes you can," said Alice. "I know it's probably too early to do this, and I shall undoubtedly be rummaging for paper clips or such like before we leave, but it will be a satisfaction to get part of the preliminaries under way at least."

So for the next half-hour, under Alice's stern and somewhat cranky direction, Johnny helped to fill the second box. Through the window he caught sight of Petit Pierre, naked to the waist as usual, working in the yard, snipping dead leaves and twigs from the major bushes. He sighed.

"What's the matter?" Alice asked.

"I sigh a lot," he said. "Weltschmerz, I guess. World pain. Or Weltanschauung, world-view, perhaps."

"You've just had a world-view of Petit Pierre out in the garden working," said Alice sardonically.

"That I have," said Johnny. "Does he know? Have you told him yet?"

Alice shook her head decisively. "No, and he must not know yet for a while. The police will tell him at the proper time. They do not want him to attack Debat, and perhaps bring about another murder."

"Speaking of violent things, and sex," said Johnny. "Did you know that in the states there is a book published that gives the deaf signs for all the dirty words that the sourdmuet — or anyone — uses."

Alice paused with a bright pink eraser in her hand, a big one. "Not really!" she said. "How fascinating. Why in the world would they want to have such a thing?"

"Easy to answer," said Johnny. "In court trials for interpreters. Rape and such like. I have a copy at home. They are all there, from — "

Alice held up a cautionary hand. "Do spare me," she said. "You might go try some of them on Pierre."

"Not I," said Johnny. "There are differences between

American and French signs, and what would be polite enough to an American might insult a Frenchman. Besides, I know only the minimal amount, in case I should run into a deaf beauty in Paris some night."

"Then it seems to be nearly utterly useless information, doesn't it?"

Johnny smiled. "Not at all," he said. "There'll come a day . . . or one might become deaf. But some enchanted evening one may find the damaged vessel of his dreams . . ."

"Everything comes if a man will only wait," said Alice sententiously.

"M'dear," said Johnny. "That's the only cliché I ever heard you say. But of course it's true."

"I didn't say it," said Alice with a bit of a snap. "Disraeli did."

"And everyone else after him," said Johnny teasingly.

She picked up a pencil and pretended to throw it at him. The phone rang.

"J'écoute," she said, picking up the handset. "Yes, Monsieur Gallos . . . it is Mademoiselle Toklas who speaks . . . We are in train of slowly beginning to prepare for our return to Paris . . . it would be possible of course . . . Perhaps tomorrow morning? No, not today, I am sorry . . . At your office at eleven? Good. You will send a car? How long do you think it will take? Yes, I will affirm to the statement willingly, but you will understand please, it would be useless for me to take a vow on a bible . . . a torah perhaps . . . Good. Until tomorrow, then."

She hung up the receiver. "Hell," she said. "Another hour away from the Permanent."

"What's the Permanent?" Johnny asked.

"Being with Gertrude," she said. "But then she may go along."

From outside, sitting in the lounge chair inhaling a rose, Gertrude had heard the telephone ring.

"Who was it Pussy," she shouted.

Alice went to the window. "The gendarmerie called," she said. "I am to see Gallos tomorrow morning. To make a deposition."

"Oh," said Gertrude and resumed her staring at Mont Blanc. It was hard being a genius, she often said — you had to sit around so much of the time doing nothing. Then she thought a moment and said, "Can I help you and Johnny."

"No," said Alice, "you know the room is too small for three, expecially with all the boxes. Besides, you're writing."

"Not now," said Gertrude. "The muse is sitting in the furrow, resting."

"She'll come back pretty soon," said Alice. "You stay there in case she needs help."

Then suddenly Alice sat down in a chair, on some old volumes of *transition*. "Damnation," she said to Johnny. "The weather is so nice. And I hate to think of going back so soon."

"I understand," said Johnny sympathetically. "And I hate to think of going back so soon, too. To the States and all those dull students. They get duller by the year."

"Gertrude told you once that you should have been a butcher," said Alice. "You will never get any writing done, using that word-finding part of your brain all the time. It's worn out by evening, and then when you try to write, nothing will come out."

"But if one has nothing to say, then one can say nothing, can one?" he said.

"You are beginning to sound a little like her," Alice said.

"I know it," he said, "but words are the same every-where. I always tell my classes that you can have more fun with them than with anything else in the language."

Alice looked at him narrowly. "How's that again?" she said.

Johnny giggled. "When I toss that sentence off to a class, the C students all write it down in their notebooks. The B students look vaguely puzzled. But if anyone snickers a little, he is sure to get an A out of the course."

"Not only bashful and blushful, you're sly and sneaky," said Alice. "As we used to say, you come in by the side door."

"Hmm-m," said Johnny, grinning. "I've never really tried it that way. How is it done?"

This time Alice did throw a pencil at him. She missed.

"Ah you," she said. "You take your double tenders and march right out into the garden with them. But you'd better not try them out on Gertrude. Translate them into French and practice on P'tit Pierre."

"Not on my life," said Johnny. He laughed and went out into the green and gold.

✿ XX ✿

Depositions and Distractions

ALICE WAS ALL TWITTERS AND JUMPINESS the next morning. She hardly listened to what Gertrude was saying.

" . . . and although I don't mind what Johnny does or with whom he does it, just as long as it doesn't happen under our roof and I don't hear about it," she finished. "Isn't that the way you feel about it, now isn't it."

"What?" said Alice, hunting among her ladythings.

" 'What' is what I always say when I don't hear what someone says but at least I say it on the third or fourth word, I don't wait until the sentence is all finished. Are you getting deaf too."

"I'm sorry, Lovey," said Alice, "but I am distracted by having to do this today and I wish it were all finished. What did you say?"

"I said — oh never mind, it wasn't important anyway. I'm going with you of course and shall we take Johnny along."

"The more souls the less misery," said Alice.

"That's what Ralph what's-his-name said about hell," said Gertrude.

"Did he?" said Alice. "What time is it?"

"You *are* distraite," said Gertrude. "There's the clock right in front of you, on the nightstand beside the bed just where it has always been for the past nine years, it's ten-forty."

"The car will be here any moment," said Alice. "Do I look all right?"

She was wearing a soft dark blue jacket suit that Pierre Balmain had sent her from Paris, and a white blouse with a string tie, and — for her — a very conservative black straw hat with a small bunch of red cherries at the side.

"Just like the Place Vendôme," said Gertrude.

She went around the corner of the bedroom into the bathroom, and through the window shouted down to Johnny in the garden.

"Will you come with us Johnny, we are all ready to leave, are you ready or not."

He waved cheerily. "Yes, I'll be glad to go along."

"We're coming down," she said. "Tell Chen to unlock the gate and open it."

Soon a somewhat battered two-door Citroën puffed up to the gate. At the wheel was Claude Oria, still almost as battered-looking as the car.

"Oh, oh," Johnny muttered to himself, "all we need now is for P'tit Pierre to come around from the garden and show himself, and there'll be another battle."

He went to the car and leaned in the window. "And how do you feel now, Claude?" he asked.

"Much better, thank you," said Claude. "Although I still resemble the very colorful sunset. Shall I come inside for Mademoiselle Toklas?"

"No, no," said Johnny, perhaps too emphatically hasty. "They'll be out in a moment."

It was one of the rare times when Alice came out of the house first, drawing on her white kid gloves. Gertrude marched solidly behind her, all in brown tweedy skirt and yellow vest, with a white blouse and tan wool stockings. Behind her pranced Basket, high-gaiting it like a Lippizaner horse, and last of all Pepe, whose yipping raised him farther off the ground than usual.

"No dogs," Gertrude addressed them firmly. "Not today. Stay and protect the house. Play fierce like yellow Hemingway."

She and Alice greeted Claude, neither of them giving the slighest indication by word, glance, or inflection that they saw anything amiss with his face, such being the crystalline impeccability of their old Victorian manners.

Then they were off, down the incline to the road to Belley. The car sputtered quite a bit and jolted them now and then.

"This machine is very sick," said Alice.

"It does not march well," said Claude. "Its illness is terminal. There is no money for a new one."

When they arrived he limped ahead of them, ushering them into the office of Monsieur Gallos where they all sat down in a semi-circle around his desk. Claude took his position at the typewriter, which looked suspiciously like the ancient Blickensdörfer that Alice had sold to the junk dealer in Belley. Monsieur Gallos twirled first one end of his mustache and then the other. A late fly buzzed against the dusty window, reminding Alice momentarily of Emily's "blue, uncertain, stumbling buzz" — a magic phrase. No time to think of her now, thought Alice.

"Will you then be so amiable as to begin?" inquired Monsieur Gallos.

"On the morning of Monday, September 13, 1937, I . . ."

"Claude," said Monsier Gallos, "please add 'the undersigned.' Your pardon, Mademoiselle."

She nodded archly. " . . . I, the undersigned, at about ten-thirty a.m. observed Monsieur Pierre Desjardins approaching Monsieur Debat . . . "

"Jean Debat," added Monsieur Gallos.

" . . . in Monsieur Debat's field where he was in train of ploughing with his horse. Monsieur Desjardins was carrying a filet of purchases he had presumably made in Belley . . . "

" . . . later verified by Monsieur Gallos . . ." said he.

" . . . and additionally verified by Mademoiselle Stein, myself, and Monsieur John McAndrews from America . . . " Alice added.

" . . . les États-Unis," murmured Gallos to Claude, who was becoming slightly confused.

"Period," said Alice. "Monsieur Desjardins seemed to be in a highly excitable state, furious in fact, a condition I could easily verify through my spyglass, which I had quickly brought from the house. Realizing that Mademoiselle Stein would also very much like to witness a confrontation which seemed about to take place . . . "

"Supposition," said Monsieur Gallos.

Alice then addressed him directly. "But the bad feeling which existed between them has been well-known in the community for several years."

"Let it stand then," said Gallos to Claude.

Alice went on. "I returned to the house to call Mademoiselle Stein, telling her to bring the binoculars so that she could watch as well . . . "

"Please state how long this took," said Monsieur Gallos.

" ... comma," said Alice, "an errand which took perhaps three minutes ... "

"Why such a length of time?" inquired Gallos.

"Mademoiselle Stein did not hear me at first and I had to repeat," said Alice.

"Please state the fact," said Gallos.

"Semi-colon," said Alice, "since she was upstairs she did not hear me the first time. I was forced to repeat the message a second and then a third time. Then I returned quickly to my vantage point and again looked through the lunette d'approche, Mademoiselle Stein joining me after about forty-five seconds. But there was no one to be seen then except Jean Debat, heading back in his field from the turn-around point at the edge of the forest, ploughing a new furrow."

"Admirable," said Gallos. "Do you have it so far, Claude?"

"Oui, monsieur," said Claude.

"Pray continue, Mademoiselle Toklas," said Gallos. "Would you perhaps like a glass of fresh water?"

"No thank you," said Alice. Then she resumed: "Subsequently Mademoiselle Stein, Monsieur McAndrews and myself conducted a small investigation in Belley, discovering that Desjardins had indeed been there earlier, and made various and sundry purchases, such ... "

"No need to mention them," said Monsieur Gallos. "The list has been twice verified."

"Very well," said Alice. "Then when Mademoiselle Stein and Monsieur McAndrews returned two days ago with a filet which they had found buried in the forest next to Debat's field ... "

"Claude, please make that September 29, 1937, instead of 'two days ago'," said Gallos.

"Bien, monsieur."

"Comma," said Alice. "I was able to identify the filet as the one I had seen carried by Monsieur Desjardins on the morning of September 13. I then informed the police, who sent an odi . . . " She caught herself and said, "one Monsieur Duvalle . . . oh, no, wait," she said in some confusion.

After a moment she went on. "I then informed the police, and the commissionaire . . . "

"Prefect," said Gallos gently.

"I beg your pardon," said Alice, "and the prefect, Monsieur Gallos, himself came to examine the filet and verify its contents."

"Excellent," said Gallos, rubbing his hands together. "It is quite perfect. But it now occurs to me, Mademoiselle Stein, that a small deposition from you and Monsieur McAndrews would be of great assistance. If you could then briefly describe your finding of the filet . . . ?"

"With pleasure," said Gertrude, who had been feeling somewhat left out.

"A new sheet of paper, please, Claude," said Gallos, waving his hand airily.

When Claude had inserted it Gallos said, "And now to begin, please"

"How fast can he type," asked Gertrude.

"Like the wind."

Gertrude took a deep breath and started off in her rather unusual French. "We were taking a morning stroll, my dog Pepe and Johnny McAndrews and I, down the hill but not on our usual path, we went instead to the forest at the edge of Debat's field, and we left Basket the poodle at home because the burrs and thistles would ruin his long-haired white coat, but Pepe did not have that problem, no, because his coat is smooth and slick, and he likes cheese and I do too but I am I because my little dog knows me and can tell the difference between cheese and me, and we went into the forest about two hundred meters, maybe only one-fifty, and suddenly Pepe began barking and digging and he dug down as far as his hindquarters with just his tail stuck up above the ground and then he found a handle which we soon saw was attached to a filet and the filet contained the camembert and the other cheap cheese that was there, the kind you use to make noodles, and we brought the filet back to the château where I live with Mademoiselle Toklas and then we called the police and here we are doing our duty and our duty now is done."

Monsieur Gallos looked stunned.

Claude's fingers had moved so fast they were almost invisible, and he was concerned with the strange grammar and syntax [certainly not the most elegant French in the world!]. Johnny's mouth had fallen open early, and stayed that way. Alice smiled.

"Did you get it all, Claude?" asked Monsieur Gallos, recovering his voice.

"Oui, Monsieur."

"Then please draw some straight lines, and perhaps each of you will sign in the proper space, n'est-ce pas?"

Done. Alice signed her page, and Gertrude the other, and then Monsieur Gallos suggested that Johnny sign beneath Gertrude's name. Claude and Monsieur Gallos then signed as witnesses.

Gertrude, Alice, and Johnny left after exchanging many amiabilities. Gallos watched them go.

"Mon dieu," he said to Claude. "How can anyone understand her at all?"

"I could," said Claude. "It all seemed to come right through my ears to my fingers."

"Without," said Gallos, "passing through your brain at all."

"Perhaps," said Claude. "But there it is."

"To be puzzled out. I fear that literature is in for a bad quarter of an hour."

"Au contraire," said Claude. "I like it. I will read more of her writing."

"Chacun à son goût," said Gallos. "The trouble is, there seems to be very little goût."

"Chacun à son goût," said Claude in turn, smiling even though it hurt his lip.

❧ XXI ❧

Night Visitors

IT WAS CLOSE TO FOUR in the morning when there occurred a
fearful noise outside the bedroom window where Gertrude
and Alice were asleep in their double bed.

Alice slept like a cat, and her eyes popped open with an
almost audible click. "Mon dieu," she said to herself, "what
can that be?"

Gertrude did not stir. She was flat on her back, nose
pointed toward the ceiling, snoring faintly. Alice slipped
from bed, seized her taffeta robe, and peered out the
window.

There were two cars outside their gate, one topped with
the little winking blue light of the gendarmerie. A double
blast on the horn of one car shattered the stillness, which
had already been sadly disturbed. Several figures, outlined
against the reflections of the headlights, were moving
around through the night fog — men, with flashlights.

"No, no," said a voice which she thought that of Monsieur Gallos. "That, that is the gate of the American women. His house is farther on. Right there," and a flash-light shone on the house of Jean Debat, up the lane a small distance.

"Lovey, oh Lovey!" Alice called and turned quickly to the bed to shake Gertrude. "Up, up, quickly!"

"Wha-what," said Gertrude thickly.

"I think the police have come for Debat," said Alice. The group had now moved on, with one of the cars; the other purred quietly in front of the château gate.

"At this hour," asked Gertrude unbelievingly.

"Just like a gangster movie from America," said Alice.

Gertrude pulled on her long blue heavy terrycloth robe and went barefooted to the window. She began to be excited.

"Oh Pussy, shall we dress a little and go down and see what's going on," she asked.

"We can see over the wall perfectly well from here," said Alice. "Down there our view would be cut off by the gate pillars. Let's stay."

They watched.

The men approached the house of Debat, three or four moving shadows. One of them knocked loudly on the door. For a moment there was no sound, and then a light went on in an upper window. Seconds later, a man's head appeared.

"What is it then that you want?" he demanded.

"You are Monsieur Jean Debat?" queried a voice.

Alice nudged Gertrude. "That awful Duvalle," she said.

"So I call myself."

"You are ordered to descend, Monsieur. We are the gen-darmerie of Belley. We would talk with you."

"For what purpose, then?"

"Descend, Monsieur. We are the law."

The head withdrew, and there came the vague sound of cursing. But a few moments later Debat opened his door, suspenders hanging down from the waistband of his pants, his underwear top unbuttoned.

"By what rights do you disturb an honest citizen at such a devil's hour?" he growled.

"Citizen, yes — honest, we shall see," said the man. It was indeed Duvalle. He produced a paper and rattled it in front of Debat's nose. "You are advised that this document is a mandate for your apprehension."

"My apprehension? On what charges?"

"On suspicion of murder."

"Murder!?"

"Indeed," said Duvalle.

"I do not know you," said Debat, looking under fierce and bushy eyebrows at the smaller man. "How do I know you are police? Perhaps you have come to rob me."

Another figure stepped forward. "You will recognize me, Monsieur. I am the prefect of police, Gallos, from Belley. It is indeed a legitimate accusation. You will please to come with us."

"I'll be damned if I will," said Debat and started to close the door. Two men holding rifles or guns of some sort stepped forward.

"Attendez, Monsieur," said Gallos in a threatening tone. "Do not force me to shoot."

Alice and Gertrude could see Debat looking from one to the other of his accusers. Then he shrugged, lifting one shoulder, and reached behind the door for his coat.

"It is all madness and folly," he said. "What is the basis for such an insanity?"

"You will discover soon enough," said Gallos. "But meanwhile be advised the we have found a filet buried, con-

taining some purchases made by your neighbor Pierre Desjardins, who has since disappeared as you probably know all
too well."

Debat muttered something indistinguishable.

"Not at all," said Gallos. "Entendu, that does not mean
that you killed him. But you were seen on the morning of
September 29TH last, about to be attacked by Pierre Desjardins."

"Seen? I? Who could have seen me — I mean, I have no
memory of seeing him."

"We have our sources of intelligene," said Duvalle.

Alice poked Gertrude. "That's us, Lovey," she said.
"See how deep we're in."

"*You're* in," said Gertrude.

"*You* found the filet, not I," said Alice.

"Oh my," sighed Gertrude. "As if we didn't have
enough to worry about. I have been having nightmares all
night. Real cauchemars, but what they were about I can't
remember, they weren't about murder, I think they were
about our being dispossessed."

"Dispossessed of what?" asked Alice.

"Dunno," said Gertrude. "Forgot. All gone."

They did not use handcuffs on Debat. Gradually they
got into the two cars, which then backed down the narrow
lane because it was not wide enough to turn around.

And soon the night was quiet again, with crickets
singing.

"A pity Johnny seems to have slept through it all," said
Gertrude.

"Ah, but he didn't," said Alice, pointing down under the
plane tree by the fountain where Johnny stood smoking,
hands thrust deep into the pockets of his maroon bathrobe.

"That one doesn't miss a trick," said Gertrude.

"Do watch your language," said Alice. "Vulgarity is for others. Besides," she added slyly, "you're wrong. He missed all of those tonight."

✤ XXII ✤

Danse Macabre

"WHEW!" SAID ALICE.

She came hurriedly in from the garden, shut the French doors behind her, and then opened them again. "He can't hear me anyway," she said.

Gertrude was sitting in her wicker rocking chair, thinking. She looked up. "Who can't," she asked.

"P'tit Pierre," said Alice. "He's in the garden working."

"That's three days running," said Gertrude. "Why is he here every day."

"There are lots of things for him to do before we leave, to get everything in tiptop shape," said Alice.

"Well, why did you say 'whew,' which you hardly ever say unless there's a crisis."

Alice peeked out the doorway. "I asked him if he was aware of the commotion last night when they took old Debat, but of course he heard nothing and knew nothing of it. So I felt that now it would be safe to tell him. And I did, I told him all about the finding of the filet."

"How'd he take it," asked Gertrude.

"Come look."

Gertrude rose from the rocking chair and approached the window. Petit Pierre was sitting on the garden wall, naked to the waist, on the far side of the pointed rake-house which was in the wall's center. He had one foot up on the wall and the other one on the ground, and had lowered his head to rest on his up-bent knee. His arms were crossed around his ankle. The golden tangle of his hair shone brightly in the autumn sun.

"He seems to be deep in thought," said Gertrude.

"He turned pale as a sauce mousseline when I told him," said Alice.

Then Pierre slowly raised his face. It was not stained with tears as Alice had thought it might be. Instead, there was an odd kind of smile on his lips. He turned his head, shut his eyes, and looked up to let the sun fall directly on his face.

"The boy *is* smiling," said Alice, somewhat awed. "He must certainly realize that the filet means his father is dead."

Pierre brought his foot down from the wall, shifted slightly and put both hands on the inside of his blue-clad thighs. He sat thus for a moment. Then with a bound he sprang up on the wall and stood facing the valley, both arms stretched wide above his head toward the sky, his back toward them.

And then slowly at first he began to make small movements with his feet, forward and back, turning his body, bringing one hand down to caress his belly, raising a shoulder. He began a little skipping motion along the length of the wall, reached the end, and then moved quickly back to the center. He jumped to the ground, ran past the center rake-house, jumped up on the other side of the wall and traversed it back and forth with the same skipping motion. On his face was an expression of almost orgasmic pleasure.

And then with great swoopings and bendings of the body, and turnings and twirlings with both arms and legs, sometimes extended, sometimes graceful as ballet movements, he started lithely to dance, first on one half of the wall, then jumping down and whirling to reach the other half, a series of complex movements, of flying arms and legs and bending body and quick movements of his head, like those of a premier danseur assoluto as he danced back and forth.

Alice was baffled. "It's an expression of pure joy," she said.

"Yes," said Gertrude, "but joy about what, because Debat was captured or because his father may be dead or what."

"It's better than Isadora," said Alice.

"And miles better than her silly brother Raymond," said Gertrude.

"But he's changing," said Alice. "Look."

And indeed he was. A kind of crouch had come into his body, and its language altered. It became static for a moment, and then slowly, like a leopard stretching, began again. But there was something wolfish, almost feral, untamed and savage about it this time — in the quick alert movements of his head and arms. He still leaped from one half of the wall to the other, running around the rake-house, but a vague threatening quality began to show, helped on by the sun momentarily disappearing under a cloud. There was a mime being enacted but neither Alice nor Gertrude could understand it. Then Pierre finally sank to his knees on the wall, spreading his legs wide, both hands clasped around an invisible neck, his thighs straddling an unseen body, and choked and choked an invisible figure.

"My God," said Alice, "whatever can be going through his head?"

"Do you remember seeing that dancer Harald Kreutzberg in Paris, now do you Pussy," said Gertrude excitedly, "when he used the long black cloak to twirl around his head and upraised arm, it gave me the same sort of chill I'm getting now."

"A real danse macabre," said Alice.

Who the dickens said anything about Micawber," said Gertrude, her mood broken.

"I didn't, you ninny — I said macabre."

"Oh," said Gertrude. "yes, it is that, it is macabre."

And then it was over. Pierre lay flat on his back on the stone wall, chest heaving. The light golden hairs on his arms gleamed in the sun, and sweat shone on his skin.

"I haven't seen anything like that before, ever," said Gertrude.

"Nor I," said Alice. "What do you suppose was going on in his head?"

"From the looks of things perhaps it's just as well we don't know," said Gertrude, "His father was mighty strict with him, and maybe he was celebrating his freedom. Or maybe there at the end he was getting even with Debat for 'dishonoring' him, wasn't that the word he used."

"Yes," said Alice. "But likely we'll never know."

"Freedom is a wonderful thing," said Gertrude.

"We have been free most of our lives," said Alice. "You got free of your family and Leo, and I got free of taking care of all those family males in San Francisco. We have both known the lack of freedom, and that was terrible."

"If the freedom of one person is taken away, the freedom of all people is. Hum. I may have to write something about that."

"Do," said Alice. "And don't forget to discuss the fact that the ones who suppress freedom always do it in the name of law and order."

"Without freedom, there are no names," said Gertrude. "Only numbers."

"My," said Alice, grinning and smoothing her dress, "we really are a pretty smart couple of women, aren't we?"

❧ XXIII ❧

Departures and Farewells

JOHNNY STOOD ALONE IN THE SALON forlornly looking around
at the dear familiar objects, the trompe l'oeil hunting horns
and cornucopia painted on the grey walls, the little clavichord in its rosewood box, the elegant Victorian table and
sofa with curved legs and back, the straight chair in which
Alice always sat, and Gertrude's wicker rocker. Since there
was no one around, he dared to sit in it for a moment and
rock.

There were four sounds he would carry away with him
from Bilignin — the solitary bird-call from the trees along
the Ain river down the hill, the tinkling of a cowbell now
and then, and the great uproar marking arrivals and departures, when Basket and Pepe added a deep-toned bark and a
furious high-pitched yapping to the shouts of Gertrude and
Alice.

But the fourth sound was the all-pervasive one, the one
that went on the greater part of the time and had fastened itself in his memory.

It was the gentle noise, the squeaking, the happy song

of the wicker rocking chair in which Gertrude always sat after dinner, during the long evenings of conversation at Bilignin. By the tempo of the sound — sometimes slow as old Time, and sometimes under the pressure of Gertrude's excitement rapid and allegro, punctuating her sentences like the commas she would have none of — he could judge just how well or poorly the evening's talk was going. The sound of the chair, as Johnny slowly rocked, was the sound of his childhood, a wholly American sound, the invisible filament that still connected him with his homeland and with his own childhood. He would take this sound with him, and it would be his as long as he lived.

It was the day of departures. His luggage sat on the floor, along with Chen's, ready to go when Gertrude and Alice took Chen and him to catch the rapido to Paris. They found that they could both leave together since they had finished all the packing for Gertrude and Alice.

He looked around the charming room, wondering when again he would see its quiet elegance and gleaming parquet floors, its worn thresholds, and the vistas out through the tall French windows. A kind of grey and sombre melancholy pervaded him. He lighted a cigarette, watching its slow blue smoke drift lazily out toward the garden.

Upstairs Gertrude was grumbling as she finished dressing. Alice looked around, trying to find a safety pin to conceal a small rip.

"I hate all this," Gertrude said. "I hate meeting trains and saying goodbye to them and waiting to meet people and then seeing them go away."

"So you've said a hundred times before, Lovey," said Alice. "Be comforted — this is the last time of the season. Suppose we still had to contend with Francis and Cecil, that would be two more times — and this is the last."

"And another thing I hate, Pussy, really more than trains," said Gertrude, "is this whole business about Debat and Grand Pierre, we didn't find the answer, and going back to Paris without knowing the solution is a little like a sneeze that keeps hiding in your head and won't come out through your nose, it's frustrating, that's what it is."

"Never mind, Lovey," said Alice. "I have a feeling that it will be solved one way or another when they find a body or when we get called back for the trial."

"When *you* get called back, not me," said Gertrude.

"You'll be called too," said Alice, "because you and Pepe found the filet."

"Hell," said Gertrude, "I betcha they won't."

"Certainly they will"

"Well," said Gertrude, "at least they can't call Johnny all the way from America." She tightened her belt another notch. "Let's get the two boys and get on the way."

Alice left the bedroom and went to the attic stairway. "Chen!" she called. "Venez mon cher, nous allons partir!"

"Oui, madame," he said, appearing at the top of the stairs.

Damn, thought Alice, I've never been able to break him of calling me that instead of Mademoiselle.

"You have everything?" she asked.

"Oui," he said, descending. He looked very slim and elegant in his dark suit and white shirt with a carefully knotted tie. "How handsome you are this morning," said Alice.

Gradually, amidst much barking from the dogs and help from Madame la Veuve Roux, who had come over to help with the closing of the château, they all got safely installed into the Matford, although Johnny had to sit with his feet up on the luggage, his knees somewhat obstructing his view of the whorl on Gertrude's head.

The trip to Culoz was made almost in silence. Johnny had planned to slip his Paris and Chicago addresses into Chen's hand, but realized there would be ample time to do that on the train, since it was always good to have a friend wherever you went. He contented himself with holding Chen's hand below the line of sight from the front seat.

And marvel of marvels, the rapido was exactly on time. They had only a five minute wait on reaching the station at Culoz. With many embraces and protestations of affection and invitations to return, Johnny got on. Gertrude in her enthusiasm even kissed Chen on the cheek, as did Alice, who pressed a five-hundred franc note into his hand. "You have aided us wonderfully this year," she said. "Perhaps if you are still at the Sorbonne you will return next year."

With grave Oriental politeness Chen bowed and said, "There is nothing that would delight me more if I should still be in France."

Then with a loud whistle and no grinding of the wheels at all, the rapido pulled out. Silence once again descended. Gertrude and Alice stood watching for a moment, and then headed back to Belley and Bilignin.

"Well," said Alice. "It's the death of another summer."

"Yes," said Gertrude, "it always makes me sad too, it's lonesome now, we're all alone."

"Do you suppose," said Alice, when they were halfway home, "that Johnny and Chen ever . . . er . . . that they ever?"

"Dunno," said Gertrude. "I suppose they did, especially after seeing Johnny kiss Chen right on the mouth in all that confusion when we were all kissing each other and saying goodbye, do you think he thought he was kissing you or me farewell, he never kissed me on the mouth and I never did him, it was a startling thing."

"Nor did he ever kiss me on the mouth," said Alice. "But then he's become more French than American, sometimes even more French than the French."

"Do you suppose he ever laid a hand on P'tit Pierre," asked Gertrude.

"No indeed," said Alice emphatically. "At least if he ever did it was one of the great triumphs of sign language, but I doubt it, considering what happened to the secretary of Monsieur Gallos."

"I still wish," Gertrude grumbled, "that we had found out what happened to Grand Pierre."

"Oh, we will, Lovey, we will," said Alice. "Sometime in the future, if not this winter then next year when we return."

A small cloud of dust followed them all the way to the château.

❦ XXIV ❦

Parisian Interlude

WHAT A WINTER IT WAS!

First of all, Basket died. The sorrow was almost too much for them to bear, and little or large tear-storms would visit them whilst they were talking, or drinking their verveine infusions, or just sitting quietly at home. Gertrude felt like getting another white poodle right away, but Picasso told her not to, since the new one would remind her too much of the old one — but that was exactly what she wanted. "Get an Afghan hound," he said, but she did not. With Alice she went one day to the Porte de Versailles and bought one exactly like Basket, who became Basket II. "That Pablo," she said to Alice — who agreed as always — "refuses to recognize continuations, but as for me, if the king is dead, then long live the king." The new Basket was afraid of stairways, but he soon got used to them.

They bought a new kerosene heater with a catalytic starter, which Gertrude did not understand at all, but Alice did. Between them, they answered three hundred and thirty-eight letters which arrived from October through December. "The postage alone is keeping us broke," Alice complained.

And then in December another blow fell, fulfilling Gertrude's earlier dream of being dispossessed. An important-looking letter arrived from their landlord. He told them that they would have to vacate their Fleurus apartment, because he wanted it for his son and new wife. Stunned, they were immobilized for several days, and then Gertrude remembered a quasi-realtor, Méraude Guevara.

"Méraude," she said to him over the phone. "We are going to have to move, the landlord wants the place for his son, will you try to help us find a new place, now will you, not too expensive and without any *bail*" — which was the sort of under-the-counter payment you had to make to new landlords for new apartments.

"But of course," said Méraude, and within three days he had found them a place on the rue Christine, a somewhat shabby little lane [Picasso had a warehouse full of paintings at the end of it on the rue des Grands Augustins], but distinguished by the fact that the wild and profligate Queen Christina of Sweden had once had her secret apartments on the same short street. Directly across from the entrance was a horsemeat shop, with an elegantly carved and gilded horse's head above the place.

They moved in the middle of January. It was horrendous — all the pictures, Gertrude's glass "breakables," the two Picasso chairs, the huge heavy Florentine furniture with the horsehair sofa that always prickled the guests who sat on it. And the books! But Gertrude accepted all offers of help in the task. She wrote to Johnny: "A nice English boy is offering to move all my books, and believe me it is a pleasure, and if you have time you should come over and help us move too."

The new apartment had fine old wainscotting, high ceilings, and parquet floors, which Alice wanted to carpet over to keep out the winter cold. But friends dissuaded her, and even paid for the restoration of the gleaming golden hardwood. The stairway to the second floor was oak, the doors were tall and firm, and Alice had bright brass plates made to announce who lived there. A mail slot was installed and the door had — as Alice proudly boasted — "the only Yale lock in Paris."

And then there began again the endless stream of visitors. It was hard for Gertrude to turn them away: the society matrons, the would-be intellectuals, the painters, the writers, the old friends, the new ones who had come with notes of introduction, the soldiers, the sailors, the waiters, the nouveaux riche, the new friends, the busboys who had waited on them, the jockeys, the students, and all the rest, countless others. "I can't find the time any more to write," she wailed to Pussy.

For all too long the new apartment was full of boxes, crates, and paintings. It seemed they would never get rearranged. They lived in the middle of a true gâchis, a tourbillion, and delayed and delayed, until finally Alice said, "I shall put away the kitchen gadgets first, together with the Mixmaster Johnny gave us."

"Yes," said Gertrude, "it has really gone on too long. If we are confronted with the insurmountable task of putting all this stuff away, then we must go at it gradually and gradually it will get done."

And she was right. They temporarily curtailed the visitors, but even so, it was well into March before all the furniture was properly placed and the pictures hung to their satisfaction, and all the knick-knack arranged just so, and the paintings they no longer liked stuck in the "Salle des Réfusées," a long corridor off the dining-room. The tables and the footstools were moved countless times, pictures hung in the bedroom and then shifted to the front. For a while the plumbing was not working properly. Alice wanted an American plumber whom she had used before, but he had moved away, and she was delighted that the French plumber she found after much searching seemed in this case to be equally as good as the American.

Besides all the visitors — taking them to expensive restaurants and to concerts and ballets — there were of course the *vernissages*. It seemed that every artist, talented or not, had succeeded that year in having a one-man show, and the invitations poured in on them, a veritable paper storm. Finally they decided they could not go to one more *vernissage*.

And then came the invitation from Francis to his opening at the Jean Bonjean gallery. It was on rose paper with purple ink.

"What awful taste," said Alice, fingering it as if it were laden with dreadful germs.

"But we will have to go, simply have to go, after we told him not to come to Bilignin last summer he will think we no longer like him or think he is any good, so we will really have to go just this one more time, don't you think so."

"I suppose you're right," Alice said.

And so they went to Francis's *vernissage*. The Galerie Bonjean was not the most attractive place in the world, and the paintings Francis had done were not up to his usual standard, so Gertrude thought. She wondered if she had been wrong in the beginning about Francis being another great painter. He himself was there of course, impeccably dressed, with a lavender ascot and pearl stickpin and an afternoon coat and a Chinese mustache, all bows and scrapings.

They bussed him soundly on each cheek, but Gertrude was forcibly reminded of Thornton's comment about his toothy semi-simian quality, and she wondered why she had really come.

The largest of his paintings was that of a woman of the Empire — or perhaps one of Toulouse-Lautrec's floozies — with bright red hat, white gloves, and a long flaming red dress. She was sitting on one of Lautrec's circular plush benches, looking for all the world like a demi-mondaine waiting for another customer. Gertrude found it very distasteful and Alice shied away from it. The title of it was *La Femme à la Robe Coquelicot.*

"Coquelicot, what's that again," Gertrude whispered to Alice.

"Red field poppies," whispered Alice. "My God, I don't think I can stay here any longer, can you?"

They looked at the rest of the paintings, most of them heads of young men, or nudes of young men in various languid and suggestive poses. "He's turning completely sexual," Alice whispered. "Somewhat like the later Tchelitchev, and you know what we felt about *him* when he did."

"Yes," said Gertrude, "and we abandonned him and perhaps we are going to have to abandon Francis and that's too bad, considering all the paintings of his we have and all that money down the drain."

"You could, of course," said Alice, "go on writing about him as you did about Picasso and saying nice things and perhaps eventually make him great, and then you could get all that money back."

"Not I," said Gertrude firmly, "and I hope you're joking. I believed in Picasso and his greatness, but if I wrote about Francis simply to get my money back I wouldn't sleep good at night and neither would you. I have to believe in a person, that's what I do, and if I don't, then I won't and I can't say anything good."

And so they went home, making many protestations of affection to Francis and inviting him to call, and with many bowings and mumblings of his execrable French, he said goodbye.

After a pot of tea at home and some of Alice's special cookies, of which Gertrude was very fond — those made with rice flour and eggs and rolled into little sausage shapes, and when cold painted with a water icing flavored with rosewater — they sat in the great high-ceilinged living room and talked about Francis's *vernissage.*

"You know," said Alice, "I don't know why but I keep thinking of that woman with the red dress. I have a tickling feeling somewhere that something about it called up, but I don't know what."

"Isn't that funny," said Gertrude, reaching for another cookie and taking a sip of tea, "I have the same feeling, I don't know why, but there's a drawer in the back of my head that feels like it should be opened somehow, it's got something in it we ought to know about, but from where and why I can't figger."

"I wonder if it had anything to do with last summer," Alice mused.

Suddenly Gertrude sat upright, nearly spilling her cup of tea. "That's it, Pussy, that's it exactly. Didn't Johnny-jump-up say something on his list about Grand Pierre buying some coquelicot seeds at the Exquisite Hardware, and what became of them, we never heard of them afterwards."

"I really don't remember," said Alice, frowning and reaching for a cookie.

"Where are those lists we all had," asked Gertrude.

"You threw yours away or lost it," said Alice, "instead

of saving it like the magpie you are. I think I still have mine."

"Where's Johnny's."

"He probably took it with him," Alice said. "You know how he saves every scrap of paper with either of our handwritings on it, what with his sense of history and how great you will eventually be."

"Let's ask him," said Gertrude. "Let's telephone him."

"Transatlantic?" said Alice in horror. "You must be mad. The cost is astronomical. No, I'll send a leter, it really won't take long with the new air-mail. About two weeks. I'll ask him to send a copy of the things he found."

"Okay," said Gertrude, "You write it right away and we'll take it to the poste and then we'll see what he says, but I'm sure I remember anyway, Grand Pierre bought some coquelicot seeds."

"Then what in the world happened to them?" said Alice.

"Perhaps he put them into his pocket with the snuff and cigarettes," said Gertrude.

"I don't see what all that would have to do with the crime anyway — what connection it would have," said Alice.

"Well, I don't either, but somehow we just missed them and that's important to me, I don't like to forget things, let's just ask him and settle it once and for all."

❧ XXV ❧

Two Letters

"DEAR JOHNNY, WE THANK YOU for your letters and for the mystères you sent, the detective stories, you know how I love them, and Alice loves all the kitchen gadgets, especially the one you keep in the frigo, the little hard piece of heavy metal that she can cool the sauces with just by sticking it in sauce, and she keeps the gadgets in the atelier on top of the most precious place, that is my manuscripts, and in her dreams she murmurs about them and the Mixmaster too, but what can the Mixmaster mix that Johnny can eat, well we will talk about that when the day comes and you are here again, won't we.

"We are still worrying and wondering about l'affaire Debat and there has been no word yet about Alice having to go back, nor me either, and now I suppose we will not have to until we really go to Bilignin again, which we are going to do by the middle of April, and then you can write us there. And we do like the new place and the new address it is lovely, 5 rue Christine, but you know that by now. Johnny we are wondering if you kept that list that Alice made, the one that Alice made when we all went to Belley to do some detectiving to see if Grand Pierre had bought anything, and he did, and we would like to have a copy of your list if you kept it and still have it, would you please send it to us if you have it and we hope you do, because we are wondering again about Grand Pierre and will wonder more when we go back down to Bilignin, so please send it, and lots of love and write soon, perhaps by transatlantic avion, I am glad they started that because letters go faster and come faster even if it costs more.

"I am writing this with a new Christmas pen, it is a monster and cost 35 francs and I bought a new camera for the same sum 35 francs and it takes lovely pictures and we will take a lot of each other and lots of love again, Gtde."

In about two weeks there came an answer:

"Darling Two, Your new address is wonderful, and do you live in the actual apartments of Queen Christina or are they somewhere else on the street? For a while I worried that the 27 rue Fleurus address, being so famous, would now not be, but then I realized immediately that the new one will become — nay, is already — equally famous just because you and Alice live there, and as time goes on it will become even more famous than 27 Fleurus. We know it will, and they will put up a memorial plaque saying so.

"They have developed a marvellous new photocopy machine and it is magic. You take the paper you want copied and put it face down on a glass plate and close the cover, then you put a coin in a slot, and a bright light edges all around the cover and the machine whirs, and then soon a paper slides out the side, and it is an exact black and white copy of the paper you want copied. So I am enclosing one of these new-fangled copies for you of the list, and you can see from my markings just what Grand Pierre bought and when. And now I must run, I have a class. I hate Beowulf because it as hard on me to translate it as it is on the students but I manage to keep at least a few lines ahead of them, and lots of love, Johnny."

"Well," said Gertrude after she read the letter. She waved the copy at Alice. "Here it is and sure enough at the Exquisite Hardware Grand Pierre bought a small paintbrush, spokes for a bicycle wheel, a paring knife, and a tenth of a kilo of coquelicot seeds. There, I knew that all along something was bothering me, and that is can anyone tell me what became of the coquelicots, did he put them in his pocket along with the snuff and the cigarettes or just what happened to them, now what."

"It would be a very small package," said Alice. "The seeds are tiny. Yes, he could have put them right in his pocket."

Gertrude stood thinking, warming herself at the kerosene heater which worked wonderfully well, except it put a faint effluvium of oil scent into the apartment, and sometimes — entering from outside — it seemed that they were walking into the garage at Belley.

Alice was embroidering on a small circular wooden frame, carefully reproducing a small unicorn rampant that Picasso had drawn for her.

Gertrude left the circle of warmth by the heater and started a slow progress around the room, around the great heavy carved Florentine table and the horsehair sofa, and then around and around again, her head sunk low on her ample bosom, the photocopy clutched in her hands behind her back.

Alice watched her, and in so doing missed a stitch. She put the embroidery hoop down with a small noise of exasperation.

"Lovey, what is it? What are you bothered about now?"

"I am thinking," said Gertrude.

"Well, so am I, but you really don't have to go tramping around the room like that, do you? Can't you think while you're sitting down or at least standing still?"

"I think better when I'm walking or at least moving around," said Gertrude. "Why don't you try it, it helps."

"Perish forbid," said Alice. "I'm quite comfortable sitting down."

Gertrude continued with her slow circling of the room until she had made about six orbits. Then suddenly she stopped.

"I am about to reach a conclusion," she said.

For the last two minutes Alice had made no stitches, her needle arrested in midair. She was looking up into one corner of the room, in a vaguely Whistlerian pose.

"So am I," she said, and put down the embroidery.

"In fact," said Gertrude. "I have reached mine."

"And I too," said Alice.

"It has to do with last summer," Gertrude said.

"And mine too."

"Tell me what you have thought, Pussy, now tell me."

"All right," said Alice, "if you'll tell me yours."

They exchanged ideas, and then Gertrude broke into a wide grin.

"If all this is true, and nothing has changed, then I believe we have solved the case," she said.

"Not yet exactly," said Alice. "It will need on the spot investigating further. Perhaps it is solved in theory but there is no evidence and no facts to be perceived yet."

"When will we leave for Bilignin then," Gertrude said.

"About the tenth of April," said Alice.

"Let's go sooner," said Gertrude. "This has been an awful winter, what with moving and all, and I am getting tired of what you call the nice fresh gasoline fumes of Paris, and more than that, I am excited to see if we are right, and I haven't felt like this in a long time."

"In that case," said Alice, "I'll go make us a pot of very strong jasmine tea and we'll celebrate."

The tea seemed almost to make them very drunk.

✿ XXVI ✿

On the Way

___

IT WAS THE FIFTH OF APRIL, a Tuesday, the second day of their trip south. They always went leisurely to Bilignin, stopping over for the first night at Dijon. The backseat was piled high with their luggage and books, and the two dogs slept as peacefully as they could on the leather-like upholstery, which Alice insisted was nothing but high-priced oilcloth.

But Gertrude was a little miffed that morning. She had looked forward to her annual glass of May wine — oh, so delicately flavored with woodruff! — at the little German café near the auberge in Dijon where they usually stayed. But they were two weeks too early, said the beaming hausfrau who owned the place.

"It's the only German thing I like and can stand," she grumbled, "and you'd think that they'd certainly have it on hand when they must know by now that I drink only one glass of it a year."

Alice chuckled. "That isn't the best bit of logic I've heard today by any means," she said. "How could they have it there for you when this year's pressing hasn't been made yet?"

"Nevertheless," said Gertrude.

"There must be other German things you can tolerate," Alice said. She was filing her nails with a delicate emery board, as usual.

"None at all," said Gertrude. "And most of all I detest, I really hate, that awful language, it's the kind of language that makes you want to fight, suppose someone came up to you and said 'Achtung, Sie sind ein Doppelgeschlechtlichkeiter!' right in your face in those horrible guttural tones" — which she mimicked very well, with at least two throatclearings and a heavy rumble — "wouldn't you feel like hitting him if you could, now wouldn't you."

Alice jumped a little at the German words. "You frighten me," she said.

"German as a language frightens everyone, it is a speech of thugs or silly paperhangers like that little Adolph, if everybody spoke Hawaiian or maybe Italian I think there wouldn't be any more wars not ever, no one could fight in Hawaiian."

Far off over the level fields they were passing just then, there hung a mist like a morning veil. As they drew closer to it, the sky darkened more, and they saw that it was a gentle rain. Gertrude turned on the windshield wipers.

"When that Aprille with his shoures soote..." Alice murmured.

"Yes, it's nice, that's wot it is, it makes things grow, and do you think it will be raining when we get there, and what time will that be."

Alice calculated quickly. "Well, with our *early* start — " she emphasized the word, for she had wanted to leave at nine o'clock but Gertrude had puttered around for more than an hour, and it was ten-thirty before they finally set off — "I think we will get there just about nine o'clock tonight, and it will be getting pretty dark by then."

"Then I'll drive faster," said Gertrude.

Alice put her hand lightly atop Gertrude's right hand on the wheel. "Lovey," she said, "please don't. It really doesn't matter, and we can spend all day tomorrow and all the other days of the summer there, but if we get killed trying to get there just before dark then we won't enjoy the summer at all, now will we?"

"You're right," said Gertrude, and eased up on the gas.

They drove on for quite a while in silence, now going directly south toward Lyon, whereas to Dijon they had been driving southeast. The countryside began to make small and subtle changes, hardly to be noticed at first — the colors grew a little riper, the grass seemed more lush, and an occasional olive-tree with lance-shaped leaves began to appear among the poplars.

"Isn't it funny in a funny kind of way," said Gertrude, "how the southern part of a country always seems more southern than the northern part of the country just south of it."

"It's hard to notice in France just now," said Alice wryly, "since there's no country south of France except the Middlesea and Africa the other side of that."

"Well you know what I mean," said Gertrude. "And anyway this trip seems longer each year we make it."

"Just as," said Alice, "all the stairs grow steeper each year, and print grows smaller, and strawberries don't taste as good as they once did, and people are talking more softly than ever before."

"When people are a little older they are knowing then that they have been younger," said Gertrude.

"That part you wrote in *A Long Gay Book*," said Alice, "which you are quoting just now — do you remember what Thornton said about it? How when he read it to people they would actually grow pale as he approached the sentence that described them as they were 'when they were a little older'?"

"Yes," said Gertrude. "That's a damned good page of writing, ain't it."

"It is indeed," said Alice. "Page twenty-five in the first edition, as I remember."

"We are growing older," said Gertrude.

"So is everybody else," said practical Alice.

"How can you remember a page number just like that," Gertrude demanded.

"Easily. It gave me as much of a shock when I read it the first time as it did Thornton."

Gertrude laughed. "As well as me who wrote it," she said. "It was scary."

"I think we'd better stop at the next wide place in the road," Alice said, "and let the dogs out for a moment. Pepe looks nervous."

Soon Gertrude pulled the car to the side under a willow tree, and they all got out to stretch. Pepe and Basket dutifully did what was expected of them. Then they went on.

"Do you suppose Madame Roux will have opened the place as you asked her to," said Gertrude.

"Of course," said Alice. "It was opened two days ago so the mustiness would go away. And she knows enough to close it at night should there be rain."

"We must not forget to notify the commissionnaire at Bourg en Bresse that we are in Ain for the summer again," said Gertrude.

"Yes, and also call Monsieur Gallos in Belley tomorrow morning to ask about Debat."

"Do you suppose he's been in jail all this time."

"Of course," Alice said. "We would have been notified about the trial."

"Maybe he's been released on bail," said Gertrude.

"I think not in this case," said Alice. "This is too serious."

"And what has happened to P'tit Pierre," Gertrude said. "And I wonder if Grand Pierre has turned up any place."

"We would have heard that too," said Alice. "As for P'tit Pierre, I suppose we'll know soon enough. Do you suppose he has married Pauline from Belley?"

"Dunno," said Gertrude. "I can still see him doing that dance up on the garden wall. After that I would be ready for anything to happen and I wouldn't be surprised if it did. Weird, that was."

It was late, very late when they arrived, and quite dark. But Madame Roux had waited for them and turned on the floodlights when she heard the car. A light drizzle was in the air.

Everything smelled fresh and clean. Gertrude took a deep breath. "Ah, this good air," she said. "I am going to sit in the garden all day tomorrow, just breathing the air."

"Not too much of it, Lovey," said Alice. "You must take it all in gradually. And at first you may miss the gasoline fumes of Paris."

"Not me," said Gertrude. "I'm just going to sit and breathe and be a genius."

"That's for day after tomorrow," said Alice. "Tomorrow you're going to help me unpack."

"Am not," said Gertrude stoutly.

Alice reached up to the corridor wall, just inside the door, and plucked the peacock feather from its hook. She reached out and tickled Gertrude's ear. "Oh yes you are," she said.

Gertrude shouted with laughter and hurried down the hall. "Oh no, Pussy, please don't. Please stop, Pussy. I'll do anything if you stop."

Madame Roux stood open-mouthed, with a suitcase in each hand, watching them as they ran through the house, turning on all the lights as they went. The old halls rang with their laughter.

Madame Roux shook her head. "Ces folles américaines," she said to herself. "Mais je les aime, tous les deux."

❧ XXVII ❧

Risks and Perils

THE NEXT MORNING ALICE STOOD looking out of her workroom window at the gentle April rain. The hectic nights of Paris were quite forgotten as she watched it. It was, she decided, the purest most-direct-from-heaven rain that she had ever seen, not so much as moving a leaf, each drop knowing its place and going to it, falling with perfect regularity.

At nine o'clock she had called Monsieur Gallos at the gendarmerie in Belley. It had been quite a lengthy conversation. Yes, Monsieur Debat was still in jail, but the prospects of trying him for murder were very dim. The judge advocate and the prosecutor were of the opinion that the finding of the filet was not sufficient to warrant a trial, and the man must soon be released. He had stoutly maintained that he knew nothing of Desjardins' disappearance, that he knew nothing of a buried filet, that the purchases — whatever they were — could have been made by anyone, that he was very likely to sue not only the police for false arrest, but also for defamation of character whoever had told them he had seen Grand Pierre in the field that morning. Alice had nervously inquired whether her identity could be [and had been] kept secret, as well as that of Mademoiselle Stein, and had been assured that it had been held in extreme confidence. And finally, it was quite possible that Debat would be released within two weeks — at the latest, the first of May. As an afterthought, she had inquired about Petit Pierre, and had been told that as far as Gallos knew, he was still living at home, next to the château.

Madame La Veuve Roux appeared in the doorway. "Where shall I put this?" she asked in her heavy patois, holding up a brand-new colander.

"I'll place it," Alice said, and went with Madame Roux into the kitchen. She stuck it in a lower door of the great cupboard and then said, "Marie-Claire, what do you hear about Petit Pierre? Is he still at home?"

"Ah yes, Mademoiselle," said Madame Roux. "He has created such a scandal. There is a young girl living with him, and they are much given to drinking, and giving nervousness to the owls with their playing of the jazz discs on a portable appareil of some species. One says that the girl is already enceinte by several months."

"I suppose it is Pauline from Belley," said Alice.

Marie-Claire's eyebrows rose above her flaming cheeks. "Indeed, of a certainty it is, mademoiselle," she said, "but how did you know?"

"It had been heard of last autumn before we departed," said Alice.

Madame Roux shook her head with its unruly wisps of hair. "It is a grave scandal," she said, "and his father if he were here — or if he is alive — would be very triste to see how his son has evolved."

"But how do they communicate?" Alice asked.

"In the beginning by notes on paper. But it is said that he has taught her the means of finger-parler, and that they now communicate like that."

"But why does he play the music if he cannot hear?"

Madame Roux shrugged. "That, it is for her ears, I think, although he can I believe sense the vibrations. And they dance together. It is an outrage of moeurs, that dancing. They have been seen through windows improperly shaded. They are barely dressed, and sometimes all naked." She shook her head in dismay.

"They are young and restless," Alice said. "They are exploring."

Madame Roux looked shocked. "It is ill-mannered of them to behave so, almost in public. In my day . . . "

Alice waved her hand. "Yes, and in mine too."

At that moment Gertrude appeared in the doorway. "It's raining," she said. "We can't go exploring today."

Madame Roux was startled. "Exploring?" she said.

"A different kind of exploration," said Alice.

She took Gertrude's arm and went with her into the living room.

"I have spoken with Monsieur Gallos," she said, and told her what information he had given her.

"Holy cow," said Gertrude. "The first of May.""

"Luckily Debat doesn't know who peached on him," said Alice.

"I should hope not," said Gertrude. "And Pierre living with that Pauline girl. Well, there goes our gardener. We'll just have to get another one somewhere."

"We'll just put you to work," said Alice.

"Not on your life," said Gertrude grimly. She looked out the French doors. "This rain will stop my walk today, but of course you wouldn't go along even if I did go."

"I hate the thought of trudging back up that hill," said Alice, "and anyway the underbrush in the forest will be simply soaked. We can't go looking for a week, even if it stops right now."

"Did you look at Debat's field," Gertrude asked. "Is the wintergrain or winterwheat or whatever it is growing up yet."

"I wanted to go out to look," said Alice, "but I decided I couldn't handle the umbrella and the spyglass at the same time. Too much juggling."

"I'll go along and hold the umbrella over both of us and you can use the lunette," Gertrude said.

"All right," said Alice. Gertrude stuck the umbrella through the French doors and opened it. Alice picked up the spyglass and they both went out into the garden. They walked to the retaining wall, and while Gertrude balanced the umbrella, Alice manipulated the spyglass into position and swept the length of Debat's field with it. The rain whispered around them.

"Is the wheat up, or the barley, or what" Gertrude asked.

"It looks green enough," said Alice, "but I can't tell how tall it is from here. It also looks as if it is overgrown with weeds. You can barely make out the lines of the furrows."

"Well, he's been in jail, he can't be down there pulling weeds."

"Nature really makes a mess of things, doesn't she?" Alice said, collapsing the telescope.

"You betcha," said Gertrude, "especially if she's left alone. Think of all the eggs that go wrong before one fish is hatched out right."

❧ XXVIII ❧

Fruitless, Indeed

THE RAIN HAD STOPPED and the bright sun of southern France had come out and quickly dried everything off. The kitchen gadgets that Johnny-jump-up had given them had all been arranged in their proper places, and Gertrude — tentatively — had resumed her daily walks. It was exactly one week after their arrival.

"I think it's now time," said Gertrude, "to go to make another little exploration, down into the woods again or just walking around."

Alice groaned. They were both sitting in the salon looking at the morning mail. The *facteur* had delivered six letters, three catalogues, and two notices of other *vernissages* in Paris. Gertrude put everything that had come to her in a small pile. Alice kept her seed catalogues separate.

"Is there anything you have that I should answer?" Alice asked.

"No not really," said Gertrude. "It's all fan mail from

some people that we must have met during the American tour. I don't remember any of them but I'll have to answer them anyway, there's an amusing letter from a Douglas Martin in Chicago, I wonder if he knows Johnny-jump-up."

"Why don't you throw all the rest of them away?"

"Not me," said Gertrude stoutly. "You know I'm a magpie, I never throw anything away, it's all there, grocery bills, advertisements, everything, it's all going to Yale to the archives, that's the way Donald Gallup wants it, and that's the way we'll do it."

"A lot of the stuff we send him every year is useless," Alice said. "They must have a whole roomful of paper by now. Just junk."

"Junk maybe, but Donald spells it j-u-n-q-u-e. High-class stuff. Historical. All part of la gloire. He and Carl think I'm a historical person. Everything must be saved."

"And is," said Alice. "The postage bill for the 1937 box of your memorabilia was over thirty dollars. And really, a lot of it was trash. What will Yale ever do with the cleaning and pressing bills, the grocery and rent receipts, the fuel bills and all the other accounts?"

"I dunno," said Gertrude. "That's Yale's problem. But think of all the fun the Ph.D. candidates will have for the next century or two, going through it and trying to find out things. The bills at Fauchon's épicerie alone will keep them busy for twenty years, trying to reconstruct our menus and discovering what caused my bellyaches, and wondering just what the hell you bought so many cornichons for."

Alice giggled. "Because I like them," she said. "And you do too."

"I'd like a pickle right now," said Gertrude.

"Well, you'll just have to wait a while," Alice said. "We

haven't laid in all our supplies yet. We'll go to Culoz one day this week and buy some necessaries. We need lots of things."

"Then I tell you what," said Gertrude. "You go put on your walking shoes and we'll go down into the woods right now, where we found the filet buried last fall, and we'll have another look around."

"The police have probably searched it all thoroughly," said Alice. "I hate climbing back up that hill. It's steep. It would have turned Newton's gravity law upside down."

Nonetheless she did as Gertrude said. A few moments later, armed with a walking stick, she came downstairs. Gertrude had picked up her sword-cane and was examining it. The narrow triangular blade looked a bit rusty.

"For heaven's sake, why take that?" Alice asked.

"Why not," Gertrude said. "I'm just taking it to walk with. You've got the shillelagh Joyce gave me and that's what I usually have."

"Shall we take the dogs?" Alice asked.

"We might take Pepe, he's a good sniffer, he might sniff out something else again," Gertrude said. "But not Basket, no not this time, the foxtails and burrs are too lively just now."

They started out. The day was serene and lovely. Great thick white rumbles of clouds lay against the horizon, and the sky was bluer than blue. They took the seldom-used path down toward the field where Debat had sown his spring crop the autumn before, and as they approached, Alice did indeed see that she had been right. The barley or the wheat (she could not tell the difference yet) was greenly shooting above the ground, but between the furrows that ran the length of the field, the weeds had begun to take over.

"When or if he gets out," Gertrude said, "he'll have a helluva hard time getting that field back in shape."

"One might think," said Alice slyly, "that if P'tit Pierre were a really good neighbor, he would have helped Debat with the field."

"After what he did . . . " Gertrude began, and then she saw the expression on Alice's face. "Oh hell now," she said, "you're teasing me, that's what you're doing. Anyway, Pierre's too busy playing at two-backed beast with his ladylove."

"Ah," said Alice, "why not call it the golden chain of rose-tinted Aphrodite?"

"It's no such thing with them," said Gertrude shortly.

They entered the edge of the forest. Pepe ran ahead of them, barking and sniffing, but not pausing to dig at any spot.

"What really are we looking for, do you suppose?" Alice asked.

"A body, I reckon," said Gertrude.

"How grisly," Alice said, shuddering.

"I supposed all the gristle is gone by now, if we find one," said Gertrude.

Alice stopped dead in her tracks. "Lovey," she said sharply, "if your hearing gets any worse you've just got to get some kind of hearing aid. It's getting terrible. I said grisly. And that little trick of yours of yelling 'What?' at everyone in the middle of a sentence if you don't hear what a person says — that really scares a person half to death. It makes him forget what he was going to say in the first place."

"And usually, nothing lost if he does," said Gertrude. "I am really getting a little tired of telling people what to think and when to think it. Anyway, hardly anyone ever listens to me, they are always too busy thinking up what they are going to say next, and even if they do hear me they usually don't believe me, and anyway I'm usually wrong."

"When it come to politics and such, yes," said Alice, "but you're always right about literature and writing and things like that."

"You're sweet," said Gertrude. "And you're right too." She walked a few paces farther. "I think I still have that long collapsible silver ear-trumpet that Aunt Pauline used, maybe I should get that out, that would be fun to use, and if I didn't feel like listening I could just lay it in my lap and all the talk would stop around the room."

"You get that out and use it and I'll go back to San Francisco," said Alice.

They went on deep into the forest until they saw the end of it approaching. Then they turned and went back in a still different direction, covering another wide swath of underbrush. Nothing, nothing. None of their poking and turning over of leaves and loam did any good. There was nothing to be seen anywhere that was the least unusual, and Pepe had found nothing. He seemed very tired, and occasionally flopped down on the loam to rest.

"Poor thing," said Alice. "We may have to carry him back up the hill. He seems so frail."

By the time they had returned to the edge of Debat's field once more, they were themselves exhausted. Gertrude's skirt had a sizeable triangular tear in the bottom of it, where a thornbush had attacked her as she bent over a large rock. She was sweating profusely, and mopped her face time and again with a large red bandana. Alice's bangs were plastered to her forehead.

"That's enough of all this," Alice said. "Let's go back. I'm completely worn out."

"Me too," said Gertrude. "But at least we tried."

Pepe made it about halfway up the hill and then collapsed. With a pitiful cry he lay down panting on the hillside and refused to move. Gertrude gave her cane to Alice and picked up the tiny dog, cradling him against her great bosom as she trudged up the hill. After a while she gave the dog to Alice and took the two canes herself.

"I'm mighty glad we didn't bring Basket," said Gertrude. Imagine having to carry him home."

She looked at Pepe nestling contentedly against Alice. "Isn't is wonderful," she said, "how all animals know that the ultimate end of life is to enjoy it."

"All animals except man," said Alice sardonically, putting Pepe to the ground as they entered the gate to the château.

❀ XXIX ❀

Quo Vadis?

"Pussy, oh Pussy, where are you," Gertrude hollered from the living room.

"In the workroom, Lovey," came Alice's voice, faint behind the closed door.

Gertrude stomped through the dining room and opened the door of the workroom. The new Tiffany lamp with its jeweled shade, a pattern of pale wisteria and red tulips, glowed beside the old typewriter. Alice sat at the table, surrounded by brilliantly colored folders of every description. In her hand she held one labeled "Spain."

"What in the world are you doing," asked Gertrude.

"Well," said Alice, "I thought it might be nice to take a little trip for a few weeks, say at the end of April."

"What on earth for. We just got here."

Alice peered at her over the top of her spectacles. "It is now the fourteenth of April," she said, "and I presume you remember what's going to happen on May the first."

"It's the day after your birthday," said Gertrude.

"No need to remind me of that," said Alice. "What else is it?"

"It's Mayday," said Gertrude, "but there'll be no maypole around this place."

"Silly," said Alice. "Of course not. But that's the day that old Debat is being released from durance vile, and don't you think it might just be wise if we were to absent ourselves from the region for a little while? Perhaps one or two years."

"Oh, I'd forgotten," said Gertrude.

"You have too many other things on your mind, Lovey," Alice said. "I'm the one to do the remembering about little things like being murdered in one's sleep."

"Do you really think we're in danger," Gertrude asked.

"Probably not," said Alice. "And probably he'll never know unless he should happen to guess who has the best view of his fields. But whether Monsieur Gallos or his Claude can keep the secret — well, why should we take a chance? And there's that horrible Duvalle. He may still be hanging around the place. He might spill the beans."

She waved the Spanish folder. "Do you remember all those years ago, Lovey, how we went to Spain and how fascinated we were with Avila? And how you wrote about Saint Teresa in the opera?"

Gertrude sat down in a chair, smiling. "Yes, I do," she said. "We had a wonderful time. And you wore what you called your Spanish disguise, the long black satin coat with the black feathered hat."

"To say nothing of the black gloves of moiré silk and the black fan," said Alice, "and good fathers, was it ever hot under all that black!"

"But how mysterious and sweet you looked," said Gertrude. "Gracious, that was — let's see — twenty-six years ago."

"We're getting old," said Alice, "No — let's change that. We *are* old."

"I'm certainly too old to go back to Spain," said Gertrude.

Alice put down the Spanish folder and fingered through the others. "Well, there's Greece," she said, "or here's Tangiers — we might go back there to see Brion or Paul and Jane."

"Too far by far," said Gertrude. "If you think we must run and hide, why not do it closer to home, there's always England . . ."

Alice shuddered. "Not on your life," she said. "I've had enough of the stately homes. Nothing but padded lunatic asylums. The British may respect your opinions but they never think of your feelings. And they think they are being virtuous when really all they are is uncomfortable. Besides, we can't go there incognito."

"We can hardly go anyplace incognito anymore," said Gertrude. "Thank God."

Alice picked up another. "There's the island of Andros in the Aegean. Or we might go to Lesbos. And," she said slyly, "bring back a native."

Gertrude flipped a paper clip at her. "The old house couldn't stand another one in it."

"The south of France? Or Cannes?" said Alice. "Bretagne? Brest? Italy? Florence? Rome? Sicily?"

"No no no no," said Gertrude. "And no."

"Perhaps we should think of going to America. Back home. We could stay with Johnny-jump-up. Or Thornie. Or Mabel."

"Johnny's place is too small, and Thornie's too much of

a gadabout. And no, not with Mabel Dodge, she's crazy by now. And anyway, I don't think we'd get the glad hand the way we did when we went over before. Times have changed."

"We might disguise ourselves and move to Culoz for a while," said Alice. "I could pretend to be an aged ballerina or give piano lessons, and you could be a ... could be a ... well, whatever you wanted to be. You could wear a false mustache and pants and play you were a traveling salesman."

"This is all tommyrot," said Gertrude. "It was enough of a chore just geting down here from Paris this year, and it gets harder every year. What do we want to go gadding about the world for anyway. We might just as well stay here and deny everything if anything ever becomes known."

"I suppose you're right, as usual," Alice sighed.

"If things get really bad," Gertrude said, "Monsieur Gallos said that he would be able to protect us."

"Hmph," said Alice.

"Maybe we could even hire Petit Pierre to stay here."

"What help would he be?" asked practical Alice. "He can't hear a thing, not even a shot. Besides, we haven't seen hide nor hair of him since we got here. He's all tied up with that Pauline he's living with."

"We'll have to find another gardener too," said Gertrude. "Maybe it wasn't the best idea in the world to come down here this year."

"Let's be patient," said Alice. "The season's just beginning, and we've got two more weeks anyway. Everything may turn out to be quite all right."

"Hell," said Gertrude. "I married a Pollyanna."

❦ XXX ❦

A Secret Agent

IT STARTED TO RAIN AGAIN and went on all the next day.

And the day after that.

And the following day. Then it turned warm and the sun came out, and on the fourth day Alice was able to take the pruning shears and go out into the garden, to try to restore some of the beautiful order which she loved so much among the little lustrous rows of box hedge, and the small rectangular plots of flowers-to-be that they enclosed.

They had decided on a small compromise. They would pack up the old Matford again, and take a week or two of holiday down on the Côte d'Azur, driving not toward the show places and the resorts of Cannes and the rest, but heading westward toward the Pyrenées and Spain. Then, if they liked it and were not too tired, they would start toward Paris in a kind of upward rising parabola, and get back to Belley and Bilignin near the middle of May. They would perhaps stop to see Picasso at Mougins if he were home and receptive [of course he would be to Gertrude, said Alice, for

had she not helped to make his reputation as the greatest of
all modern *artistes*?]

"It's a good plan," said Alice, after they had decided. "It
will give us a chance to see a few old friends, not many, and
to enjoy the lovely sight of the Middlesea. It's really been
years since we've been on the Côte d'Azur."

"What about food along the way," Gertrude asked. "You
had better get out all the good food guides and make a list of
the places where we can get decent meals and I can keep an
eye on my diet."

Alice waved a sheet of blue paper in the air. "I'm ahead
of you, Lovey," she said. "It's already done. And there are
lovely places to eat down there. Thornton gave us some
names and Madeleine and several others. It will be not only
a hegira, but a gourmet's pilgrimage."

"A hegira, wot the hell's that," Gertrude demanded.

"Any flight made for the sake of escape or safety," said
Alice. "Originally, the flight of Mohammed from Mecca to
Medina, hence the . . ."

"All right, all right, I get it," grumbled Gertrude. "I just
hope everything works out all right for us." She wiped her
forehead with her bandana. "Whew. It's turned really warm,
for so early in the year."

"Yes, it has," said Alice.

"Are we going into Belley today," Gertrude asked.
"There's a lot of things we ought to buy before we start."

Alice waved another piece of paper at her. "Ahead of
you again," she said. "I have made a list."

"Let's go right now, Pussy," Gertrude said. "If you're
through in the garden."

They called the dogs and got into the car and drove to
Belley.

The shopping took them almost two hours — needles,

thread, gants de toilette, soap, buttons, a dear little case of miniature tools that caught Alice's eye — containing a small screwdriver, a bottle opener, a corkscrew, and a tiny wrench. Gertrude refused to go into The Exquisite Hardware because of the presence there of Mademoiselle Guerre, until Alice came to the door and signaled her that the old woman was not there that day.

But it was a mistake to call Gertrude in, for although each one of them could enter a store of gadgets and go directly to what was wanted, and buy it and leave, when both of them went in together a mysterious kind of doubling occurred — and neither of them could leave without handling almost everything in the shop that glittered. "It's the magpie in us," said Alice.

"More like the packrat," said Gertrude.

Eventually, however, they left the hardware store and stepped into the brilliant sunlight of the square.

"Look," said Gertrude, "isn't that young Claude what's-his-name, the secretary to Monsieur Gallos."

"It is indeed," said Alice, putting two fingers in her mouth and letting go with a shrill blast that suddenly stopped all the traffic around the square, and made everyone look in her direction. She waved to Claude, summoning him.

He came across the square smiling, and shook hands with them. He was wearing a splendid grey suit with a dark maroon tie. His hair was carefully combed and waved.

"I am enchanted," he said, "and honored to see you again. Monsieur Gallos said that you had returned for the summer months."

"You are looking healthy and elegant," said Alice. "We trust you recovered from your unfortunate accident of last year."

For a moment he looked blank and then he smiled again. "Completely, mademoiselle."

"We were wondering," said Gertrude, "whether you could tell us anything about Monsieur Debat and his approaching release."

"It is all decided," said Claude. He had had a front tooth replaced with a gold one, which glowed in the sunlight. "Monsieur Debat will be released on May the second which falls on a Monday."

"What is he going to do then?" asked Alice.

Claude lowered his voice. "In strict confidence, mademoiselle," he said, "it sounds as if he is going to sue the whole of the Third Republic — all of the officials in Belley, the Ministry of the Interior, everyone he can think of, and I suppose even myself. He has a dishonest lawyer from Marseilles, in whose eyes there shines the light of millions of francs."

"Has he by any chance," said Alice, "been able to discover who it was who saw him in the field with Pierre Desjardins?"

Claude raised his hand as if swearing an oath. "Believe me, mademoiselle, no one knows. It is the best kept secret of all. Only three persons are aware — Monsieur Gallos, Duvalle from Culoz, and myself. And we have told no one, especially not the advocate for Monsieur Debat."

"Bon, bon," said Alice with relief. "Do keep us informed of any changes, will you? Mademoiselle Stein and myself are going to the southland for a week or two of rest, and will be leaving soon."

"Ah, yes," said Claude. "And do you get word from Monsieur McAndrews? Is he well?"

"He is well and happy and healthy, and sends you his deep affection," said Gertrude.

"If you should desire it, young man," said Alice, "we would be pleased to have you call on us some afternoon this week, for tea."

"I should be delighted, mademoiselle," Claude said. "And might I be so bold as to bring a volume of Mademoiselle Stein's to have her sign it for me?"

"Indeed you may," said Gertrude beaming.

Then bending, Claude brushed Alice's hand with his lips. He shook hands with Gertrude. "I will give you a coup de téléphone soon," he said.

"Good," said Gertrude. They watched him saunter across the square. "What a charming young man," she said.

"Isn't he," Alice agreed. "And it is always good to have the acquaintance of a double agent. I wonder if he knows that we know that he and Johnny-jump-up had a little fling together?"

"You can bet your billabong he does," said Gertrude. "I saw it in his eye."

❧ XXXI ❧

Gules on a Shield Vert

"OF ALL THE SILLY THINGS that we seem to have got ourselves into," grumbled Gertrude the next morning, as she went on packing. "It seems that we just got here for the spring and summer, and I was not going to do anything except sit in the garden and write and breathe the good air of the Bugey, and here we are, packing up again, and goodness knows for how long, and I'm sorry we ever saw, or rather you ever saw, Grand Pierre going after Debat that morning."

Alice held some brown leather-wrapped curlers, of the sort that ladies used long ago to put curls in their hair.

"Yes," she said, "I know, and it is a bother, a real bother as you say, but we might as well not tempt the Fates. Will you be needing these curlers on the trip?"

Gertrude snorted in exasperation. "Wherever did those come from anyway and where did you find them," she demanded. "You know perfectly well that I haven't used any kind of curlers for years, ever since you cut my hair and I've been wearing it this way. No, of course not, I don't need the curlers, throw the damn things away."

"Now Lovey," said Alice soothingly, "don't get rambunctious and go off in a tizzy. I know it was a stupid question. I wasn't thinking. We are both under a good deal of pressure, it would seem. And it will really do us good to get away for a little while. Forgive me for not thinking straight."

"All right, all right," said Gertrude. "Yes, we are under pressure, a lot of it, and it's something I don't like at all, it may bring on another block for me just when I was beginning to enjoy writing my pages."

"The vacation will bring even better results," said Alice. "When we get back you will double your output and get even more done than before."

"Sometimes I wonder what's the use," said Gertrude. "Nobody wants to publish my serious stuff anyway, just the sort of memoir things I did for your autobiography and then also for the second volume of it."

"Ah, don't worry, Lovey," said Alice. "Some day someone will publish everything you've ever written and there will be volumes and volumes of it."

"Do you really think so, Pussy," said Gertrude. "I do need consolation and support every once in a while. People make so much fun of me."

"Of course they will publish it all, and of course people will make fun of what they don't understand, because they feel they have to attack to make themselves feel superior. Don't worry, everything will come out all right."

"That makes me feel better," said Gertrude. "I can always depend on my Alice."

Alice looked around the room. "Have we got everything we need from here?"

"I think so," said Gertrude, "except my pills and they're downstairs in the diningroom."

"Let's go down then and look around and see what we should take from there."

Each of them struggled with a suitcase down the steep stone stairs.

"Lord, mine seems heavy," said Alice.

"Mine too," said Gertrude. "You'd think we were going around the world."

They went into the salon to look around. "How about reading material?" Alice asked.

"I've got two Dashiel Hammetts in my suitcase," said Gertrude. "We can always buy stuff along the way if we have to or want to."

Suddenly Alice saw the spyglass on the clavichord. "I think I'll take that along too," she said, heading for it. "By the way, did you pack your binoculars?"

"I forgot 'em," said Gertrude. "I'll go upstairs and get them. We will certainly need them down in that country, there's too many wonderful things to see."

Left alone, Alice gently caressed the leather and brass fittings of the beautiful lunette, and then a sudden thought came to her. "I believe I'll just check Debat's field once more," she said to herself. "What with all the rain and warm weather ... "

She stepped through the tall French doors into the garden. The day was bright and lovely, the sky intensely blue. As she walked toward the garden wall she slowly extended the telescope until it was at its full length. When she reached the wall she looked briefly down in the valley ...

... and gasped aloud in surprise and astonishment!

Even without the spyglass she could see it, there at the far end of Debat's field — a large oval of bright scarlet glowing at almost the exact center end of the field — a burst of brilliant red set against the pale translucent green of the young shoots that were everywhere waving in the gentle wind.

She was trembling so hard she nearly dropped the instrument. And there was no question of being able to hold it steady enough to look through it. Kneeling, she rested it against the edge of the stone wall.

Yes — that's what they were — poppies! From the seeds which Grand Pierre had undoubtedly stuck in his pocket, and which could not be found elsewhere. All winter they had lain dormant, and then the rains and the sun of April had made them rise!

It must have been a very shallow grave he dug, Alice thought — and then turning she screamed as loud as she could.

"Lovey, oh Lovey, come quick! Come down here into the garden at once!"

Gertrude stuck her head out the bathroom window.

"What on earth's the matter, Pussy," she demanded.

Alice was so excited that she hopped a little, and swung the spyglass in a wide arc. "You can't see from there, the tree's in the way. Come on down here. There's something — oh, how exciting!"

In a moment Gertrude hurried across the garden gravel. "What is it, what do you see," she asked.

Alice pointed. "There in Debat's field," she said. "Look! Look!"

Gertrude looked. "Well, I'll be . . . I'll be . . . hornswoggled," she said. "Coquelicots, as I live and breathe!"

Alice put the spyglass down on the garden wall and seized Gertrude's hands in hers, and swung her partner around in a dizzy small circle, dancing and hopping with glee. Gertrude danced with her, and then exhausted and panting after a moment, they fell into each other's arms and hugged mightily. Then suddenly Gertrude stopped.

"Just what the hell are we celebrating," she asked. "There's a dead man buried down there, I betcha, and here we are acting like a coupla schoolgirls. Let's go right in and call Monsieur Gallos. What is today anyway."

"The twenty-ninth of April," siad Alice. "How can you forget? Tomorrow's my birthday. And we were going to leave tomorrow morning."

Gertrude, sobered though she was by the realization that Grand Pierre, friend and neighbor, was probably down in the field, nonetheless allowed herself a large smile. "So," she said. "That's just the way we thought it might be solved after we saw Francis's painting in Paris, and now it is, and it was the poppy seeds after all. I guess we are about the best there is, ain't we."

Alice nodded happily. "And there's one thing that's wonderful about it," she said. "We don't have to go on our little trip."

Gertrude groaned.

"What's the matter?" Alice asked. "You didn't really want to go anyway, did you?"

"No," said Gertrude.

"Then why all the groaning?"

"You know if there's any one thing I hate to do it's pack. And if there's anything I hate worse than packing, it's unpacking."

"Just this once," said Alice, "I'll do it all for you."

Gertrude groaned again.

"Now what's the matter?" Alice said.

"I just remembered," Gertrude said, "that I forgot to get you a birthday present."

❧ XXXII ❧

Is It, Then, All Over?

IF LIFE IN PARIS could be said to run at a speed of, say, a hundred kilometers an hour, then life in the leisurely pace of Ain in the Bugey might be said to march at a lazy eight or nine. But for the next few days the speed increased until it nearly rivaled that of Paris.

Alice called Monsieur Gallos at once that morning, and told him that a matter of great importance demanded his presence at the château at once, and asked him to bring a team of stong-shouldered helpers with shovels to dig, dig, dig.

"May one inquire the purpose?" asked Monsieur Gallos. Alice could picture him twirling his great mustache.

"We believe that we have found the body of Monsieur Desjardins," said Alice calmly, while Gertrude stood beside her, or rather danced beside her, for she was unable to stand still with all the excitement.

Alice replaced the receiver in its cradle. "What did he say, Pussy, what did he say," Gertrude asked.

"I believe he may have exploded," she said, grinning.

In not quite thirty minutes a car pulled up outside, men with shovels descended,, and Alice and Gertrude pointed out to Monsieur Gallos the patch of poppies growing in the field far below. Then they stood in the garden by the wall as the men, running and sliding in great haste, made their way down. By that mysterious telepathy that follows all news of consequence, gradually most of the twenty people of Bilignin found their way to stand silently on the hilltop beside the château and watch the proceedings below.

"How do you suppose they found out," Gertrude asked.

"We're on a party line, remember?" Alice said.

Then a few cars began to arrive from the town and by noontime the little road from Belley had ceased to be a thoroughfare, packed as it was by arriving vehicles. By noon there must have been a hundred persons gathered on the hillside.

They found the remains. This was one part of the drama from which Gertrude and Alice turned away. When they looked again, the men had unfolded a stretcher and were struggling back up the hill with it. On it lay a black bag of vaguely human shape. Most of the carriers, and Gallos — who climbed behind them all — had handkerchiefs tied over their noses, or were holding them over their lower faces. Gallos, his face all red from exertion, stopped to see them, while a *flic* from Belley attempted to clear away the cars of the onlookers so that the police could get back to town.

"It was a wonderful exercise in logic, deduction, and intuition that you two great ladies have done," Gallos said, mopping his perspiring face. "You have brought lustre and much praise to yourselves."

"Thank you," Gertrude said. "It is a sad day for all of us

but we were glad to be of service and assistance. Mademoiselle Toklas and I have been . . ."

Gallos interrupted her. "You are great detectives," he said, "and we will see to it that all credit goes to you." Then he looked around. "Where, perhaps, is the son, the deaf-mute?"

Alice said, "I believe he has barricaded himself in his house."

"I shall want to speak to him later," said Gallos. "Would you be so kind as to interpret my questions to him?"

"I shall be happy," said Alice, with a faint inclination of her head.

"We will now go to the medical examiner at once," said Gallos. "I will let you know the results as soon as they are known to me."

And he was true to his word. Early that afternoon he called. It was indeed the body of Desjardins; he had been identified. He had been killed by a sharp instrument, probably a spade turned sidewise, that had left a great slice through his skull. Debat's release had been canceled, and further questioning had brought his full confession, although he had claimed self-defense.

Then it all really began. First, the newspaper *France-Soir* called from Paris, and had a lengthy telephone interview with Alice, followed by *L'Humanité* and even the staid *Le Figaro*. Within the next week all the newspapers in France, it seemed, had sent reporters to see Gertrude and Alice, who were forced almost daily to turn the garden into a place for a news conference with the journalists. Both of them spoke on *Radio Française*, interviewed by eager and respectful men and women. Reuters news agency put the story on the international wire, and calls came even from New York and Chicago.

All of the elements of the classic *crime passionel* were there, and the French press, in its most sensationalized purple prose, took full advantage of them: the dishonored and helpless deaf-mute son, the angry father, the farmer-lover who killed [justifiable self-defense, said his lawyer], the new young "bride" — pregnant as could be — it was a heyday, a field day, for the sentimental sob-sisters of the press to pull out all the stops of passion, unholy love, murder, and horticulture [an expert on poppies came from the Ministry of Agriculture in Paris]. And the part played by Gertrude and Alice received full attention [even Johnny-jump-up in Chicago was drawn into it, because of his discovery of the purchase of the seeds], with Alice always managing to insert the names of Gertrude's major and available writings into every interview, and placing herself in the most humble and un-exalted position. And it was Alice who interpreted for young P'tit Pierre — although *France-Soir* sent its own linguist to finger-parler with him as well.

It was the first time Gertrude and Alice had seen young Pierre since their arrival in early April. He looked remarkably healthy, handsome as ever, and seemed not overly depressed at the sad news about his father.

"And what do you intend to do now?" he was asked by a pimply flat-heeled young Amazon from a scandalous paper in Paris.

"I have been tending my father's vineyards," Pierre said, with a downcast and pious look.

"You will then stay here?"

"Yes. My bride and I will live on our land, for where else would we go? And our child will soon be born." He gave an adoring glance at his "bride," now swollen with seven months of child.

And so it went. Daily the stream of visitors came to

overlook the field where the body had been, and the trampled scar at the end of the field, for the earth had not been replaced. Alice kept the gate to the château firmly locked after a while, and at last refused to be questioned by the curious or interviewed by the press. Gertrude had early retired to her upper room to begin writing the story of the murder, but almost as if by some infernal judgment, no sooner had she picked up her new pen to begin than the block descended on her again, as short and sharp and decisive as if the blade of the guillotine had chopped off her talent. Sighing, she began to doodle, and ruined nearly an entire fat notebook before the block finally and gently withdrew. By then she was interested in Doctor Faustus anyway, almost to the exclusion of all else except eating.

It was a double nine-days' wonder, and after the eighteenth day, almost as if by magic, the phone stopped ringing, the cars stopped arriving, and no visitors knocked at the gate.

The trial was set for midsummer, in July. Both of them would have to testify, and the story would have to be told once more.

"Good grief," said Gertrude. "That means it'll start all over again."

"No cloud without its silver lining," said Alice.

"Such as what, in this case," Gertrude demanded.

"Have you forgotten, Lovey, the letter from your agent about the reprinting of the Autobiography? And the twenty-three percent increase in the sales of your work that he reported? And the paperback reprints that Peristyle asked about?"

Gertrude stroked the back of her head. "That's right," she said, beaming. "And there's been so much going on that I had really forgotten. Wouldn't it be great if every two months or so people would want to know about it all over again, and then we could go on selling things like wildfire. Or perhaps we could find that someone in Hollywood wanted to make a movie of it. Or maybe even we could find another murder to solve."

Alice shuddered. "Bloodthirsty," she said.

"Nope," said Gertrude. "Just practical."

✿ XXXIII ✿

Not Really. . .

AND SO THE MONTH OF APRIL with its green buddings passed
into the sweet month of May. The good life at Bilignin settled down into the gentle somnolence once more, although
nothing was seen of P'tit Pierre, who seemed to have abandoned them forever, preferring the pleasures of the goose-
down bed and the warm coverlet. What sensual delights
took place in his shuttered house, or what new positions for
the book of love were created, no one knew.

Gertrude and Alice went on their calm and casual way.
The block having been lifted, Gertrude spent her mornings
composing, and life seemed pleasant once again, although
over them hung the ordeal of July when once more their
quiet privacy would be shattered at the trial. Now and then
a random guest arrived, but that seemed not to bother them
much.

But it was really ruptured on June the fourteenth, unex-
pectedly. On that night, engaged in talking to a minor poet
from Jackson Hole, Wyoming, they heard a feeble clatter at
the iron bars of the front gate.

"Who in the world . . . " said Alice, rising to go out.

"Shoo them away," said Gertrude. "It's too late for anyone sensible to be calling. Tell them to come back tomorrow."

Soon Alice returned. Leaning on her shoulder was a skinny girl of about eighteen with fantastically large breasts and a belly big as a basketball, her dark hair disheveled, her dress torn, and bruises evident on her thin arms. Both eyes were blackened, and she was weeping with great dry sobs.

"My God," said Gertrude. "Who's this."

The boy from Wyoming was speechless.

"This," said Alice, patting the girl's shoulder, "is Pauline, the companion of P'tit Pierre."

"What does she want," demanded Gertrude, "at this hour especially."

"But look at her," said Alice, lapsing into French, of which the willowy boy from Wyoming understood not a word, save for a cliché he had once learned in high school, which went "Voulez-vous coucher avec moi ce soir?"

"She has a tale to tell," said Alice, "that may freeze the porches of our ears."

Gertrude stopped rocking. "Vraiment?" she said. "Alors, then we shall hear it."

And so, fortified by some brandy which Alice brought her in an elegant snifter, with many sobbings and interruptions to blow her nose, Pauline told her story.

It would seem, it was revealed, that she could no longer live with P'tit Pierre. And why was that? He beat her, he drank, he sat for long hours moody and with fingers quiet, not finger-parler-ing a single word, and he wanted nothing but a sheath for his sword, all the time, every day, every night, time after time. And just this night she had heard from him — even drunk as he was — a story so horrid, so incroyable, that she thought she might not be able to tell it ever again. But pressed gently by Alice and Gertrude with motherly tones, she began.

Pierre [she said] was a villain — an arranger, a fixer, a manipulator . . .

"Ah," said Gertrude to Alice in English, "as we had once surmised." And then to the girl again, "Continuez, s'il vous plaît."

Pauline went on. He had hated his father with an unholy passion, hated the rules, the commands, the orders, the way he held P'tit Pierre in bondage almost, permitting him none of the freedoms which all young men have and so ardently desire. And in the secret linings of his brain he had concocted a plan. With sorceries and flirtatious eyes he had looked on Debat, and enticed the robust farmer — wifeless, and with strong urges — into thinking he would accept his amorous advances. And on a fatal night when his father was away, Pierre had lured Debat into a field, and with the pretense of being very drunk on Debat's green brandy, had permitted himself to dishonored in the basest way.

Then, still bleeding, he had told his hot-tempered father, who after thinking about it a little had gone to attack Debat and beat him senseless.

Breathless, Alice whispered: "The morning that I saw him."

Gertrude nodded, and said to Pauline, "Pray continue."

Petit Pierre did not know what happened, only that his father had disappeared. But he suspected. And then the two great demoiselles américaines had found the filet, and Pierre was overjoyed and started to drink more and more. And shortly after he had gone to Belley for Pauline, taking her back to live with him.

"The danse macabre that we saw him do on the wall,"

Alice whispered again. "Patricide! He was killing his father!"

But — Pauline went on — Pierre still did not know what had happened to his father, nor that he had been killed. It was only when the two American ladies had discovered the tell-tale of the poppy-seeds — which everyone else seemed to have missed — that the crime had been resolved.

"And he told me all this while he was drunk this evening," sobbed Pauline, "and then he beat me, and said I must live with him forever, and that he would kill me if ever I told anyone. But I must leave him."

She looked up at them with tear-stained face. "C-could I stay here the night?" she asked. "I fear for my life. I will leave in the morning, and go to my aunt in Culoz."

"We will take you to Culoz," said Gertrude, getting up from her rocker and putting her arm around the thin shoulders. "You can sleep upstairs."

"In Chen's room," Alice added, and after a little while they tucked her in bed, and Alice brought warm wine, and the girl fell asleep.

Still talking French they returned to the salon, where the boy from Wyoming sat with wide eyes.

"What can we do about this," asked Gertrude.

"Nothing, absolutely nothing. No court would convict him. He did not kill his father. He only arranged it."

"Could it be called a conspiracy," Gertrude asked.

"That takes two," said Alice. "And who was the other one? Nor could he be termed an accessory either before or after the fact. Nor an accomplice."

"What can be done," Gertrude asked.

"Nothing," said Alice. "He will go free as a bird. And for our own safety we had better not tell anyone."

They sat for a long while, thinking. The willowy boy from Wyoming fidgeted in the silence.

"What in the world is this all about?" he finally asked.

Gertrude looked at him with a vast irritation. Then she reverted to English.

"Why in the goddamned hell don't you learn French," she said. And then, coldly, she said, "Come Pussy, let's go to bed."